Praise for
SHOOTING KABUL

"This is a worthwhile book about the immigrant experience in general, and Afghani culture specifically. Fadi is a likable hero who learns from his mistakes, and whose talent allows him to make a unique contribution to finding his sister, for the inevitable happy ending."—SCHOOL LIBRARY JOURNAL

"Beginning in the months before 9/11, this sensitive, timely debut follows an Afghan family's emigration to San Francisco. . . . [Senzai] writes with powerful, realistic detail about Fadi's family's experiences, particularly the prejudice Fadi finds at school after planes hit the Twin Towers and the guilt he suffers over Mariam's disappearance."—BOOKLIST

"The tale is also compelling, and the compassionate portrayals of Fadi and his family (who are eventually reunited with their lost daughter) will keep readers engaged."
—THE BULLETIN OF THE CENTER FOR CHILDREN'S BOOKS

"In N. H. Senzai's debut novel worlds collide and a little sister is lost. Can her big brother find her from half a world away? At the same time, how can he find himself and restore his honor in a land that is both foreign and home? Turn the pages. Find out."
—Kathi Appelt, author of THE UNDERNEATH, a 2009 Newbery Honor Book

"The hero of SHOOTING KABUL starts life in the United States as a foreigner, but by the end of the book, young readers will be cheering for Fadi as a good friend."—Mitali Perkins, author of SECRET KEEPER

"Senzai has brought a whole new world to life for young readers. It is a world they won't soon forget."—Reza Aslan, author of NO GOD BUT GOD

"Senzai has captured a moment in recent history with enormous grace, skill, and emotion. A powerful read."
—Ahmed Rashid, NEW YORK TIMES bestselling author of TALIBAN

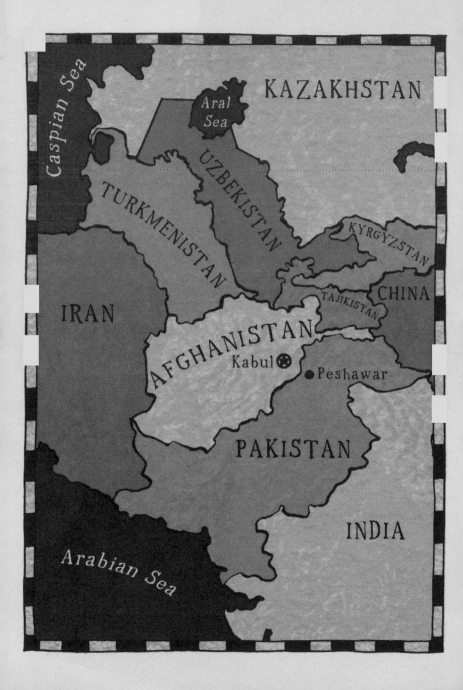

Shooting KABUL

N. H. Senzai

A Paula Wiseman Book
Simon & Schuster Books for Young Readers
New York   London   Toronto   Sydney

SIMON & SCHUSTER BOOKS FOR YOUNG READERS
An imprint of Simon & Schuster Children's Publishing Division
1230 Avenue of the Americas, New York, New York 10020

SIMON & SCHUSTER BOOKS FOR YOUNG READERS is a
trademark of Simon & Schuster, Inc.
For information about special discounts for bulk purchases, please contact Simon & Schuster Special Sales at 1-866-506-1949 or business@simonandschuster.com.
The Simon & Schuster Speakers Bureau can bring authors to your live event. For more information or to book an event, contact the Simon & Schuster Speakers Bureau at 1-866-248-3049 or visit our website at www.simonspeakers.com.
Also available in a Simon & Schuster Books for Young Readers hardcover edition.
Book design by Lizzy Bromley
Map illustration by Drew Willis
The text for this book is set in Bembo.
Manufactured in the United States of America
0817 OFF
First Simon & Schuster Books for Young Readers paperback edition July 2011
16 18 20 19 17
The Library of Congress has cataloged the hardcover edition as follows:
Senzai, N. H.
Shooting Kabul / N. H. Senzai.
p. cm.
"A Paula Wiseman book."
Summary: Escaping from Taliban-controlled Afghanistan in the summer of 2001, eleven-year-old Fadi and his family immigrate to the San Francisco Bay Area, where Fadi schemes to return to the Pakistani refugee camp where his little sister was accidentally left behind.
ISBN 978-1-4442-0194-5 (hc)
1. Afghan Americans—California—San Francisco Bay Area—Juvenile fiction.
[1. Afghan Americans—Fiction. 2. Refugees—Fiction. 3. Emigration and immigration—Fiction. 4. San Francisco Bay Area (Calif.)—Fiction.] I. Title.
PZ7.S47953Sh 2010
[Fic]—dc22
2009041148
ISBN 978-1-4442-0195-2 (pbk)
ISBN 978-1-4442-0196-9 (eBook)

For my Pukhtun and a half,
Farid and Zakaria

Contents

Shooting
KABUL

Getaway

IT'S A PERFECT NIGHT *to run away*, thought Fadi, casting a brooding look at the bright sheen of the moon through the cracked backseat window. It reminded him of the first line of the book *From the Mixed-up Files of Mrs. Basil E. Frankweiler.*

"Claudia knew that she could never pull off the old-fashioned kind of running away."

Fadi was only halfway through the first chapter, so he didn't know how successful Claudia had been in her getaway, old-fashioned or not, but he sure hoped that his family would be. If they weren't, they were going to be in an awful lot of trouble.

Under the protective cover of darkness, the taxi he and his family were traveling in swerved around a bombed-out Soviet tank and exited the pockmarked highway. They needed to avoid the checkpoints set up by black-turbaned men on the main road. With the headlights turned off, the car careened over a rocky plain, rattling the passengers' teeth. Fadi pressed his nose against the cold glass, peering across the desolate landscape.

His reflection flashed back, revealing a thin face with unruly dark hair escaping from beneath a traditional beaded cap. His nose sloped slightly to the left, evidence he'd broken it once. He held his breath when the driver nearly hit a tree stump while plowing through a parched wheat field. Another mile and they arrived at the outskirts of the sprawling city of Jalalabad, in the eastern province of Afghanistan.

The driver slowed, weaving his way through narrow alleys toward the crumbling buildings that rose in the distance. They bypassed quiet residential neighborhoods and a shuttered local vegetable market. Finally, the brakes squeaked in protest and the taxi came to a lurching halt alongside a row of deserted warehouses. The concrete walls were riddled with bullet holes and grenade blasts.

"Is this it?" asked Fadi's father, leaning forward in the front seat.

"Yes, Habib. We're on the corner of Jalalkot Road and Turi Street," replied the driver.

Habib peered at the corner, his lips compressed in a tight line.

"As a boy I remember coming here with my father," added the driver with a heavy sigh. "For generations the merchants here created beautiful handcrafted paper."

Fadi took in the desolate junction, trying to imagine bustling streets, shops overflowing with stacks of gleaming paper, customers haggling over prices.

"All right, then," said Habib, his voice quavering for a moment. "Let's go."

"Come on, Fadi, snap out of it," whispered Noor, Fadi's older sister. She pushed open the door and stepped out first, followed gingerly by their mother.

"Zafoona," said Habib, turning to his wife, "are you all right?"

"Yes," said Zafoona, her voice a thin whisper.

Noor took her mother's elbow and gently propelled her toward the side of the road.

Fadi emerged next, keeping a protective hand on his younger sister, Mariam, who slid out behind him. The faint moonlight provided just enough light to help guide them into the sheltered doorstep of a shuttered tea shop nearby. Noor and Fadi's mother stood enveloped in burkas, two smudges of light blue against the drab gray walls.

Fadi glanced back and saw his father push a wad of cash toward the frail white-haired taxi driver, who shook his head. After a heated whispered discussion the driver finally pocketed the money and opened the trunk so that Habib could pull out their meager belongings. Fadi eyed the two scuffed suitcases. Most of what they'd owned—the plush carpets, color television and video player, radios, jewelry, fine china, toys, clothes and even his mother's beloved books—had been sold on the black market, or used as bribes to get their paperwork and passports in order.

"*Salaam Alaikum*, and good luck, Habib," whispered the driver. His eyes glanced nervously over the deserted, dusty street.

"*Walaikum A'Salaam*, Professor Sahib, and thank you for risking your life to bring us here," replied Fadi's father with a grim smile.

"How could I not?" replied the driver. "You were my best student in Kabul University," he added, cracking a tired smile.

"That was a long, long time ago," said Habib, giving the man a fierce parting hug.

The family said their good-byes and watched as the

taxi disappeared down the road, its broken taillight fading into the gloom.

Fadi peered down the empty street, trying to make out the words on the broken signs lying on the dusty pavement. ZAKARIA'S PAPER EMPORIUM read one, while another claimed to have the finest writing vellum in all of Afghanistan.

The eerie stillness was broken by muffled coughing as Zafoona covered her mouth with a handkerchief. Before she could tuck it away, Fadi saw a trace of blood on the snowy white cloth.

She is getting worse, he thought, worry creasing his forehead. He glanced at his father, who gave him an encouraging wink and gently squeezed his shoulder. Fadi smiled in return, but he could see the fear lingering in his father's eyes, fear coupled with determination. As a Pukhtun, his father was bound by the ancient, sacred code of Pukhtunwali to protect his *namus*—the women of his family—with his life. With a shiver Fadi recalled the moment, nearly six months before, when his father had revealed his plan.

It was a blustery day in January as the family sat together at breakfast, trying to keep warm under layers of clothing. Fadi's mother set down a plate of old bread she'd reheated, along with chunks of white cheese, a rare treat.

"Ooooh!" said Mariam. Her hazel eyes sparkled as her fork inched closer to the plate. "Something to go with boring old bread. . . . Come to me, my yummy in the bummy tummy." At Zafoona's nod she speared a large sliver.

"Hey!" squawked Noor in mock anger. "Leave some for us." She poked Mariam in her ticklish spot, under the ribs, and got a loud giggle.

"I only took a tiny, tiny piece!" squealed Mariam, and wiggled out of the way.

"Girls, behave yourselves," said Zafoona, casting them a weary disapproving glance.

While Mariam spread cheese on the bread, her expression turned serious. She glanced at Noor with pursed lips. "Hey, Noor," she said in a loud whisper.

"What, Ms. Yummy in the Bummy Tummy?"

"I need your help with something."

"With what?"

"Will you teach me how to sew Gulmina a new dress?" Next to Mariam's plate sat a Barbie that was the envy of all her friends. She'd inherited Gulmina from Noor when her older sister had outgrown it. And now, even though the doll's features had faded and she was missing her left hand, Gulmina accompanied Mariam everywhere.

Noor took a piece of cheese and looked at her younger sister with a raised eyebrow.

"Please, please, pretty please?" begged Mariam. "I'll do your chores this whole week—peel the potatoes and turnips, take out the garbage, and iron the clothes."

"I don't know . . . ," began Noor. "You're not even allowed to use the iron—"

"Please," cried Mariam. "I'll do whatever you want." She put on her sad puppy-dog face and flashed two dimples at her older sister.

"Oh, all right." Noor sighed. "I guess there's nothing better to do than design a new wardrobe for Gulmina the Glamorous."

"Sure," said Mariam eagerly. She chattered on about what colors to use, mostly lavender and pink, while braiding Gulmina's patchy honey-colored hair.

Fadi tuned out his sisters' phenomenally boring conversation, added a chunk of crumbly brown sugar to his watered-down hot milk, and stirred. He watched fat snowflakes swirl through the crisp air and land in the backyard. He shut his left eye and pretended to look through the viewfinder of his father's old camera, which Habib had given to Fadi for his eleventh birthday, a few months before. He squinted, framing the old plum tree against the cloudless blue sky. He wished the weather were better. Maybe he could have convinced his father to take him to the quiet back hills of the city to take pictures. But, no. It was too cold—and too risky—to be caught with a camera. His eye fluttered open as his father cleared his throat.

"I have something I need to tell you," said Habib.

Fadi glanced away from the accumulating snow with a frown. His father didn't sound like himself.

"The situation has become too dangerous for us here," said Habib. There were deep circles under his eyes, as if he hadn't slept for many nights.

"Situation." That's an understatement, thought Fadi as he resumed stirring his milk. Over the past year things had gotten more and more frightening. Even going out for bread could get you in all sorts of trouble.

"And so it's set. We are leaving," announced Habib, looking around the table.

"Leaving?" Fadi mumbled, blinking slowly, like a confused owl.

"What?" said Noor, as her fork dropped with a loud clang.

Zafoona sat calmly. It was as if she had been expecting the news.

"Father, what do you mean. we're leaving?" asked Noor.

Even Mariam, who'd been busy scraping out the last of the honey from a metal tin, paused to stare at her father. "*Why* are we leaving?" she asked, her brows knitted in confusion.

"Your mother needs better medical care," said Habib.

Fadi glanced at his mother's pale face. She sat shivering, cold despite wearing two sweaters, one of Habib's old coats, and a shawl. She'd caught a cold at the beginning of winter and it had gotten worse. The few doctors left in Kabul didn't have the right equipment to diagnose what was ailing her or the right medication to make her better. She'd taken a turn for the worse the week before when they'd buried her mother, Fadi's grandmother, in the cold, hard ground next to her husband.

"It's because of *them*, isn't it?" said Mariam, her eyes wise beyond her six years.

They all knew who she meant—*them*, the Taliban.

"Yes, *jaan*." Habib sighed, reaching across the table to ruffle Mariam's fine reddish brown hair. "The Taliban have made it very difficult for us here."

Zafoona cradled her steaming cup in her hands. "It had to come to this," she murmured, muffling a cough.

"You were right, Zafoona *jaan*," Habib said with a deep sigh. "We shouldn't have come back."

"You only had the best intentions for the country . . . for the people," said Zafoona. She patted her husband's hand. Her face was laced with sadness and a trace of pity.

Mariam frowned, looking from one parent to the other. "What do you mean, 'We shouldn't have come back'?"

"Mariam *jaan*," said Zafoona, giving her youngest daughter a resigned look. "Remember I told you we used to live in America?"

Mariam nodded. "Father went to university there to get his P . . . PH . . . PH something."

Noor wrinkled her nose. "PhD, silly. Doctorate of Philosophy in Agriculture."

"Yeah, PhD," said Mariam, grimacing at Noor's know-it-all-ness.

"You were born in America, in Wisconsin," added Noor.

"But why did we come back to Afghanistan, then?" asked Mariam, her sticky fingers drumming against the table, the honey tin forgotten.

"Father and Mother wanted to help the people in Afghanistan," said Fadi, trying to shut her up. He wanted to know more about how they were going to leave.

"And you did help them? Right?" prodded Mariam. Zafoona's lips tightened at her impertinence, but she stayed silent.

Fadi rolled his eyes. Mariam somehow managed to get away with everything.

"Yes, *jaan*," explained Habib, as if trying to remember it all himself. "When we returned to Afghanistan, the Taliban asked me to help get rid of the country's vast poppy fields that were used to make drugs."

Fadi had heard this all before, how Afghanistan had become the world's largest producer of opium and how the heroin derived from the poppies was ruining the country.

Mariam nodded uncomfortably. She had seen the thin, ragged drug addicts huddled on street corners, begging for scraps.

"Slowly I convinced the farmers to destroy their poppy plants and start growing food for the hungry people," said Habib.

"Your father worked very hard," interrupted Zafoona, "but things didn't work out as we'd hoped."

Fadi looked at his father's defeated expression with growing apprehension. His father had always been optimistic, even during the most difficult times.

"But if the Taliban did such a good thing, why are they bad now?" asked Mariam.

"Mariam," said Zafoona, her tone full of warning.

"It's all right," said Habib, holding up a weary hand. He turned to Mariam, his expression solemn. "It's human nature, Mariam *jaan*. Whenever someone is handed lots of power, they have a tendency to abuse it. The Taliban was a group of young religious students. When they first came to power, they brought peace and order to the country. But with time their strict interpretation of Islam began suppressing the people they'd helped free."

"That's why they made you grow a beard," Mariam said, and smiled, reaching out to stroke her father's face.

Habib laughed. "Yes, they did, didn't they? But what they don't see is that you cannot force someone to be religious. It must come from their heart."

"It's not fair," burst out Noor. "The Taliban is oppressing everyone, with a version of Islam that they've cooked up. They've banned everything! Music, movies, books, photography, and kite flying. Show me where it says that in the *Qur'an*. Show me!"

Fadi knew that wasn't the main reason she was upset. Although many women in Afghanistan traditionally chose to wear the burka, a head-to-toe covering—including his grandmother and his aunts—the Taliban now made it mandatory. Women were compelled to cover up when they ventured outside. Worst of all, they'd closed down the girls' schools, saying the schools would reopen when stability and safety had been restored to the country.

Zafoona murmured, "Oppression is the worst thing in Allah's eyes. He forbade it not only for himself but also for us."

"True," said Habib, "but unfortunately, the world is full of oppression—oppression of men against men, group against group, and nation against nation."

Fadi sighed. Life in Afghanistan had become more and more dangerous for their family, especially since the Taliban's most recent visit to their house.

"Where are they?" grumbled Noor, interrupting Fadi's thoughts. She tapped her foot and pulled back her burka, revealing flashing brown eyes under arched eyebrows.

"They should be here any minute," Habib said in a soothing voice.

Fadi pulled Mariam under the tattered awning as she tried to inch toward a skinny dog nosing through a pile of garbage. She hadn't spoken a word during the white-knuckled six-hour ride from their home in the capital city of Kabul. Now she clutched Gulmina at her side and looked up at Fadi, a frown marring her usually cheerful round face.

"It'll be great, you'll see," he whispered. "There's lots of chocolate where we're going. And Barbies," he added with a grin.

She nodded, fingering the bright pink burka that enveloped Gulmina. Noor had sewn it for her just the week before, during a fit of boredom. The Taliban had banned all toys that depicted human figures, since they were considered sacrilegious, so Gulmina was hidden away in the folds of the bright cloth. "If you say so," murmured Mariam.

"I do say so," said Fadi, ruffling her hair. He sensed that Mariam knew they were never going back to their sprawling villa on Shogund Street, with its airy rooms and plum trees in the backyard. Well, only one plum tree. Since the war, the trees had been cut down for firewood. And after years of neglect and lack of money for repairs, the house was falling apart.

"Remember," whispered Habib, pinning an especially stern gaze on Mariam, "under no circumstance are you to tell anyone your real name. If anyone asks, tell them we are farmers escaping the fighting in our village."

Mariam nodded with a gulp. She'd been warned

repeatedly not to reveal who they were or they could be arrested and taken back to Kabul.

"And, Fadi, pay attention. We won't have a lot of time once the truck shows up."

Fadi nodded, straightening his back.

Habib glanced down at his wrist, but it was bare. He'd given his watch to their faithful servant, Shamim, that morning as they'd left the house. "What time is it, Noor?" he asked, pulling thoughtfully on his white-streaked beard.

"Seven minutes past midnight," replied Noor, glancing down at her glow-in-the-dark Mickey Mouse watch with the frayed strap.

A braying donkey rounded the corner, its owner in tow, causing the family to shrink against the building, trying to disappear into the shadows. Fadi peeked around the cement wall to watch the one-legged man pet the long-eared animal. Fadi closed his left eye and imagined the scene through his camera's viewfinder. There was something sad yet endearing about the image. Many men, women, and children had lost limbs to land mines across the country. Fadi blinked, his eyes watery. For all the problems in Afghanistan, this was still home. Dread crept into his heart. Would this be the last time he ever saw it?

"Oh, Rosebud, my lovely four-legged friend," coaxed the man. "Let's go home so you can have potato peels for dinner."

Rosebud tried to bite her owner, causing Mariam to smother a giggle.

Fadi smiled and shrugged off his morose thoughts. His mind wandered back to Claudia and her great escape. *We need to be successful in ours.* He didn't want to imagine what the Taliban would do to his father if they were caught.

2
Lost

AT 12:42 AN ARMY GREEN TRUCK rounded
the corner and stopped a few blocks down the road. Its
canvas top ruffled in the wind as it paused and shut off
its lights. Habib stepped out from the shadows to get a
better look, but without warning the truck revved its
engine and drove off, disappearing around the corner.
Muffling a curse, Habib returned to his spot next to his
wife, who sat on a wooden crate Noor had found.

Fadi held on to Mariam's skinny arm while tightening
his grip on his backpack. Everything he owned was in
that bag—a change of clothes, the family photo album,
his Matchbox cars, an old honey tin, and his camera,

the old Minolta XE. At the last minute he'd thrown in his ragged coverless copy of *From the Mixed-up Files of Mrs. Basil E. Frankweiler*. It was the only book he had been able to save from being sold.

Since the banning of books, people had resorted to illegally trading them on the black market. Every few months Fadi would accompany his mother and Noor to a carefully chosen location arranged by a bookseller whose renowned shop had been raided and shut down. After digging through piles of old books, they'd quickly make their purchase. Within minutes they'd emerge onto the road and head home, the books hidden in bags under piles of vegetables.

The bookshelf in their living room at home now held only an assortment of religious bound volumes and his father's periodicals on agriculture. All the family's other books—the thick novels, compilations by the great Afghan poet Rumi, children's books, and magazines—were stashed in the unused chicken coop in the backyard, next to the lone plum tree that hadn't been chopped down for firewood. It was the tree Fadi had fallen out of when he was eight, when he broke his nose.

"Fadi," whispered Mariam, poking at a pile of soggy paper with a stick she'd found. "I'm bored."

"Me too," said Fadi with a sigh. "Be patient. We'll leave soon."

"Shhh!" hissed Noor, glaring at them.

Fadi was in the process of giving her a cross-eyed I-dare-you-to-hit-me look in return when they heard the rumble of an engine coming from a side street.

"Hush, all of you," scolded Habib, peering down the street.

Two orbs of bright light reappeared where the green truck had disappeared.

Fadi tensed. *There it is! The same truck.* It revved its engine and slowed down. The truck traveled a few blocks farther from the tea shop, then sat idling, as if waiting for something. Or someone.

Habib stepped forward and squinted at the row of numbers printed on its side. "Three-two-nine-three-eight," he whispered, then checked a scrap of paper in his hand. "Quickly," he ordered, grabbing the suitcases. "Fadi, take Mariam."

This is it, thought Fadi, his heart racing. His father had paid human traffickers twenty thousand dollars, the family's entire savings, to get them out of Afghanistan into neighboring Pakistan. But they wouldn't stop there. They had a long, dangerous journey ahead of them. He took Mariam's hand and hurried toward the truck.

Noor followed, half carrying, half dragging their mother toward the truck while Habib picked up the suitcases and followed.

Gripping Mariam's hand, Fadi avoided a pool of stagnant water and circled a heap of rusting metal parts.

"Where are we going again?" breathed Mariam.

"To Peshawar," whispered Fadi. "It's a city on the border of Pakistan and Afghanistan. Remember Mother told you that her cousin lives there? She and her husband run a clinic for refugees, and they're going to meet us at the border."

"Oh," replied Mariam, clenching Gulmina as Fadi dragged her past a narrow shadowy alley.

Fadi paused next to a burned-out car for the others to catch up. Noor and his mother came up beside them, and then a loud splash echoed on the right, followed by the sound of running feet. A group of men ran in front of them and veered toward the truck. Two women with three small children emerged from behind an oil drum near the truck and scrambled onto the back of the truck.

"Hurry," yelled Habib, his eyes wide as he staggered past. "We have to get on that truck."

Dozens of people emerged from hiding places, all scrambling toward the truck. Fadi and Mariam followed

Noor, bypassing a group of women carrying an old bearded man with sunken, tearful eyes.

"Come on, you two," Noor shouted over her shoulder. She half lifted, half pushed their mother ahead, elbowing past two teenage boys with bundles under their arms.

Pushy as always, thought Fadi, tightening his hold on Mariam's hand.

He tugged, but Mariam didn't budge. *What the . . . ?* He looked down to see her fumbling with Gulmina. "Come on, Mariam," he grumbled.

"Wait," she pleaded, trying to tuck her Barbie under her sweater.

"We don't have time!"

"Can you put Gulmina in your backpack?" she asked, holding out her precious Barbie.

"No, not now. We don't have time," Fadi turned back to the truck, dragging Mariam behind him.

"Noor!" echoed Habib's voice from up ahead. "Bring your mother this way." Habib had thrown the suitcases onto the back of the truck and had clambered on board. He spotted Fadi and waved at him to hurry, then turned his attention back to Noor as she reached the truck. Habib leaned down and wrapped his arms around his wife as Noor pushed from below.

He pulled Zafoona over the railing and helped her inside.

With his eyes trained on the spot where his father had disappeared, Fadi started to run. Mariam clung to his hand, gasping for breath, trying to keep up. Habib reappeared at the back of the truck, and Fadi saw him reach down to pull Noor inside. He was about thirty feet from the back of the truck when a family in stained, torn clothes tumbled out from the warehouse next to them and pushed ahead.

"Ouch!" cried Mariam, losing her balance as one of the unkempt boys knocked her over.

"We've got to hurry!" cried Fadi, wasting precious seconds to pull her up. His heart raced. He couldn't see Noor or his father. He grabbed Mariam's sweaty hand and pushed through the mob.

The old man they'd passed earlier lay on the muddy street, surrounded by the women who had been carrying him. They were sobbing, talking to themselves, trying to figure out how to get the exhausted man on board. *He doesn't look good,* thought Fadi, feeling a pang of regret. But he couldn't help them even if he wanted to, so he scurried on, straining to see over the heads of the two girls at the edge of the crowd.

There he is!

Habib was a few feet away, standing on the truck's bumper, combing the crowds. His eyes widened as he saw Fadi. "This way, Son!"

Fadi spotted a gap between two women in burkas and dove in. *Only a few more feet and we'll be on the truck.* He'd reached the rear tire when a panicked scream tore through the crowd.

"It's them!" shouted a fearful voice.

The crowd constricted around the truck, plastering Fadi and Mariam against the back tire.

"Who?" yelled someone from the truck.

"I can't breathe!" cried Mariam.

"The Taliban are here!" repeated the first voice.

The sound of tires squealed in the distance, back toward the tea shop.

Screams sounded at the edge of the crowd, and people began to push, struggling to get on board. Three men climbed on top of the truck, hanging on to the cables that fastened the canvas roof to the metal sides.

"I'm leaving now!" shouted the driver, his voice a worried growl.

Fadi inched around the back as strong hands reached down to grab his shirt. "I've got you!" cried Habib.

"Ouch!" cried Mariam, stumbling as she clung to Fadi's hand.

"Hold on to Mariam!" ordered Habib as the truck revved its engine.

"I have her," shouted Fadi, glancing back at his father.

Habib started pulling Fadi up. "Keep a tight grip," he said. "I'm going to lift you both up."

"Gulmina!" cried Mariam as Fadi jerked his face toward her.

He saw a blur of bright pink fall to the ground.

"We can't leave her," said Mariam, twisting sharply.

"No!" cried Fadi, reaching out with his other hand to get a better grip, but he missed. Instinctively he clung to Mariam's hand, but her sweaty little fingers slipped through his just as the truck rolled forward and picked up speed.

Habib jerked him up just as she crumpled to the ground.

"Father," he cried in desperation, "let go." He tried to pull free of Habib's grasp, but he was already on the back of the truck.

Father and son looked at each other in horror as the truck raced up the alley, leaving stragglers behind. Mariam was swallowed up in the dispersing crowd, a tiny little girl in a sea of strangers. Screams filled the air as a black SUV made a U-turn near the burned-out car and closed in behind them. Men with long beards and crisp turbans hung off the sides, pointing in their direction.

The driver hit the gas and the tires squealed as the truck made a sharp turn and then accelerated right through a bombed-out warehouse onto a parallel alley. Fadi looked from the edge of truck's railing in disbelief. His six-year-old sister had been lost because of *him*.

3
Asylum

FADI CLENCHED THE BOARDING TICKET in his fist and stared out the small round window. An expanse of feathery white clouds floated in the turquoise sky. *From the Mixed-up Files of Mrs. Basil E. Frankweiler* sat on his lap, but he hadn't read a word of it. The words kept swimming around beneath his eyes, not making much sense. With a shuddering sigh he closed his eyes, leaned back in his seat, and tried to think of something else . . . anything else. But he couldn't. The hot ember of guilt burned in his mind, and his thoughts flew back to the night of their escape.

· · · · · · · · · · · · · · ·

Habib's anguished face appeared, begging the truck driver to turn back. But the frightened driver didn't stop. The Taliban were in hot pursuit, and he had a lot of money riding on getting his human cargo across the border. At first Zafoona didn't understand what was going on, but her pale face whitened further as Noor told her what had happened.

Zafoona sat in shock, and then she screamed, "Nooooooo!" The raw sound reverberated through the back of the truck. With superhuman strength, she lunged toward the back flap, but Noor held on to her. "We have to go back! My baby, my baby is there!" sobbed Zafoona. As illness and exhaustion overcame her, she crumpled to the ground. "She's all alone. . . . She's only six!"

Fadi could hear the echoes of her anguished wails as she pleaded to the other passengers to stop the truck, to go back to find her little Mariam. But the others looked away. They couldn't stop, or they would all be arrested, or worse, killed. Noor held on to her mother's sobbing body, trying to comfort her as best she could, her horrified gaze flying from her father to Fadi. Habib tried to climb out of the truck, but the other men wrestled him to the floor. He would get himself killed—either from falling off the truck or by the pursuing Taliban.

Fadi sat huddled in a corner replaying over and over again the instant his fingers had left Mariam's hand as the truck accelerated to a breakneck pace, finally losing their pursuers in a side alley of Jalalabad's maze of streets. From there the driver drove off the main road toward the border. By the time the truck reached Pakistan, Zafoona's cries had ceased to an exhausted whimper. Habib still clung to the back railing, watching Afghanistan disappear behind them.

His father's shame flowed over Fadi as the other passengers looked at Habib with pity. Habib's *ghayrat* was in tatters. He had lost his sense of honor because he had not been able to protect his *namus*—his daughter.

But it wasn't his fault, thought Fadi. *It was mine. I have no honor. I didn't protect Mariam.*

Fadi opened his eyes and glanced to his right. Noor slouched next to him, complimentary earphones jammed into her ears. Fadi winced. The intense rhythm of drums and the discordant clang of cymbals could be heard from his seat, and he wondered if she was going to go deaf. But Noor didn't seem to notice. She sat staring down the aisle with an intense frown on her face. In her lap sat a fashion magazine she'd picked up at London's Heathrow Airport, where they had caught their flight for the final leg of their journey. The magazine was open to a spread showing a model hiding in a tropical forest, dressed in shades of coral, resembling an orchid. Noor hadn't turned the page since they boarded the plane hours ago. Across the aisle Fadi eyed his parents. Zafoona slept, slumped in her seat, while his father reviewed the forms they'd received from the American consulate in Peshawar.

The papers had been waiting for them, arranged with the help of Habib's old college adviser in the United States. Stamped on them was the word "asylum." The consul at the U.S. embassy had explained that the U.S. government allowed refugees to come to America if they were in danger in their own country.

We certainly were in danger, thought Fadi, watching his father's long fingers gently refold the pages. Fadi recalled the chilly night when the family had sat down for their evening meal and the Taliban had found Habib.

"Turnip stew again?" complained Mariam. "That's three days in a row."

"Don't complain," said Zafoona. "There are thousands

of children on the streets who don't have even a piece of moldy bread to eat."

Mariam crossed her arms over her chest and sat with her cheeks pooched out.

"Come, *jaan*, eat," cajoled Habib. "If you finish, I believe there is a jar of plum jam left. Wouldn't that be nice on a piece of bread?"

"Don't spoil her," said Zafoona with a glower. "No treats for you, young lady, until your food is finished."

Mariam had just picked up her spoon when there was a loud knock at the front gate.

"Are we expecting guests?" asked Habib. His forehead crinkled.

Zafoona shook her head. Her eyes widened and she leapt up from her seat. "Children, upstairs now."

"Shamim," Habib said, and turned toward their servant. "Open the door and see who it is."

Instead of hiding in his room as he'd been ordered, Fadi crept down to stand at the top of the stairs. With his face pressed between the balusters, he watched a line of dark turbans file into the house, met by Habib, his back straight and tense.

Shamim hurried to get tea for their guests while the group exchanged pleasantries and settled down on the cushioned floor of the living room. Fadi inched down the stairs as far as he dared to listen to the fragmented conversation trickling up to the second floor.

". . . your family is greatly honored in Afghanistan," said a young, gruff voice. "We have heard heroic tales of how your brothers fought against the treacherous Soviets and helped defeat them."

"One died taking out a KGB command post," came another awed voice.

"Yes, yes," murmured Habib's soft voice. "My brothers were honorable men who fought and died for their country . . ."

Fadi couldn't make out the rest of his father's words, and he leaned forward, nearly losing his balance. Another inch and he'd have tumbled down the steps.

"You are a proud Pukhtun, like most of our Taliban brothers," murmured a deep, commanding voice. "You did a great service by getting rid of those poppy fields."

"It was my honor to rid Afghanistan of opium, brother," responded Habib.

"Now we need your help again, Brother Habib," said the gruff voice.

"A man with a Western education like yours could provide great service to our country," continued the commanding voice.

"What do you mean?" asked Habib.

"You studied in the United States, did you not?"

"Well, yes," replied Habib. "I received my PhD in America."

"Ever since we took power, foreign governments like the United States and France have said they will not recognize our authority to rule Afghanistan. Once again, we've been called to come before the United Nations to present our position. You could help us. You have lived among the Americans and know their ways. As our ambassador, you could convince them to accept our rule."

Fadi sat back in shock. *Join the Taliban? As an ambassador?* He leaned over the banister, practically hanging upside down so he could hear his father's answer.

"Brothers, you honor me greatly," replied Habib. "But I am not a leader or a politician. I am just a teacher at heart. I don't think . . ."

Fadi frowned. He'd lost the rest of his father's words. *Talk louder!* He was about to tip over when he felt a sharp pinch on his butt.

"Get up here, you little brat!" Noor whispered in his ear. "Do you want to get Father in trouble?"

Grumbling, Fadi retreated to his room.

As soon as the Taliban left, Fadi, his mother, and

Noor hurried down the stairs, followed by Mariam, who sleepily rubbed her eyes.

"Go to bed, Mariam," urged Noor.

Mariam shook her head. "I'm part of this family too, you know," she grumbled. "I want to know what's going on." With a huff she followed them down into the living room.

Over the next half hour, Zafoona's cheeks grew pale as she paced back and forth while Habib described what had happened. "Oh, my goodness," she said, wringing her hands. "This is terrible, just terrible."

"I know. What a pickle." Habib sighed, tugging at his beard. "The Taliban have become an irritation to foreign governments."

"Well, taking in Osama bin Laden and his trouble-some friends doesn't help their cause," said Zafoona.

"But the men at the bazaar said Osama was a good friend to Afghanistan," piped up Mariam. She'd created a fort made from cushions and was looking out of the opening. "He fought against the Soviets and saved us."

"Oh, brother," muttered Fadi. *Mariam is going to get it.*

Habib smiled. "Yes, Mariam *jaan*. Osama bin Laden helped us fight against the Soviets. The United States even gave him money during the war. But unfortunately he is using that friendship for his own gain, and the Taliban feel obligated to help him."

"But, why?" asked Mariam.

"Our Pukhtunwali tenant of *melmastia* dictates that we do not turn out a guest once we have given them our hand in friendship and a place at our table."

"Oh, Allah, have mercy," replied Zafoona. She collapsed onto a chair and wrung her hands. "What are you going to do?"

"I can put them off for a while," said Habib. He ran a hand through his rumpled hair. "I'll figure a way out of it."

"There is the smell of war in the air," said Zafoona ominously. "The Northern Alliance is bringing together warring factions to resist the Taliban. Shamim was telling me the rumors he overheard in the market."

Fadi and Noor exchanged a worried glance. The Northern Alliance, led by General Ahmed Shah Masood, a great warrior during the Soviet war, was made up of non-Pukhtun Farsi-speaking groups. Many of the groups didn't get along and were led by corrupt warlords with unsavory reputations.

For a moment Habib's face twisted in frustration. "In the end they all want to grab power for themselves," he said in disgust.

Unlike his brothers, who had joined the army after

high school, Habib had gone to the university. He didn't believe in war, or that violence was the way to solve problems. His dream had always been to rebuild Afghanistan and bring peace to its people. Fadi could see the disillusionment in his father's eyes.

"What are we going to do?" asked Noor, speaking up. She looked from her father back to her mother.

"We should have stayed in Madison," muttered Zafoona.

Fadi had heard the argument before. While living in the United States, Zafoona had watched the news coming out of Afghanistan with growing concern. It had been in the spring of 1996, and Mariam had just been a year old. The Taliban had risen from eastern Afghanistan and had marched through the country, slowly gaining control.

"Are you sure we can't stay in the States, Habib?" Zafoona had asked.

"*Jaan*, my student visa runs out in a few months and we have to leave," Habib had told her. "I could try to find a job here—that would extend our stay—but don't you think it's our duty to go back? We are educated. We can help the country get back on its feet after so many years of war. I can help the farmers improve their crop yields, so fewer people will be hungry. You can open a school, like you've always wanted to."

Zafoona had pursed her lips in contemplation as Habib had pushed on.

"Just last night CNN was showing the Taliban's visit to the United Nations headquarters in New York. They are an amazing group of young men—inexperienced, sure, but they are bringing law and order to Afghanistan. They're getting rid of all the corrupt and brutal warlords that took over the country after the Soviets left. Many refugees are returning." Habib had coaxed, "In your new school you could teach the kids all about the great books you love so much."

Zafoona had smiled and relented. She knew her husband was an idealist, and in the end she'd agreed to his plan. Deep in her heart she'd also wanted to see her mother, whose health had deteriorated while they'd been in Wisconsin. Within a year of their return to Kabul, Habib's dreams had been shattered. The Taliban took control of the capital, and Kabul University was closed. The black-turbaned young men banned the education of girls, and any hope of Zafoona's opening a school was erased. The once respected and honored Taliban became what they were fighting against, the oppressive warlords and dictators that had preceded them. When the Taliban gave Habib the ultimatum to join them, Habib knew the family could no longer stay.

The flight attendant interrupted Fadi's dark thoughts as she stopped her cart next to them. Noor snapped out of her daze and pulled out her earphones.

"We have two options for your meal today," said the flight attendant with a white-toothed smile. "Chicken with pasta or fish over rice pilaf."

Fadi looked at her blankly for a few seconds; his brain was slow in getting used to English again, even though his mother had drilled them every day during their homeschooling. *"Chicken"? What is "chicken"? Oh yeah,* charg. "Chicken, please," he said.

"Chicken," responded Noor. "Please," she added as an afterthought. She pushed Fadi's elbow off the arm-rest. "Stop hogging my space."

Fadi quickly moved his elbow. He didn't want to provoke her. She was in one of her *moods* again. The flight attendant gave them their trays and turned to his parents.

"Two fish, please," said Habib, lowering his and Zafoona's tray tables.

As Habib took the steaming trays of food, Zafoona

opened her eyes. She was a little better after the medicines the doctor in Peshawar had given her, but she was still weak.

"Try to eat, *jaan*," whispered Habib. "You need to keep your strength up."

Zafoona rolled back the tinfoil and eyed the fillet of fish lying on a small pile of yellow rice. As she picked up the fork, her eyes filled with tears. "How can I eat when I don't know if my baby is hungry or not?" she whispered.

Deep creases lined Habib's clean-shaven face. "She will be found," he said.

"You could have gone back to Jalalabad again," said Zafoona.

Fadi watched his father's face sag. "I didn't find anything, *jaan*. There was no trace of Mariam, or anyone who'd seen her. I barely snuck back across the Pakistan border with my life. I had to bribe the border guard with the last of our cash."

Fadi dug his fingernails into his seat. The four days his father had been gone had filled them with constant fear. If the Taliban had caught him, he would have ended up in jail, or worse. It wasn't till he'd returned, dirty and exhausted, that the family had breathed a sigh of relief. But he hadn't found a trace of Mariam.

"We should have stayed in Peshawar, then," said Zafoona, turning her face away from the food.

"We couldn't, *jaan*," said Habib patiently. "We'd delayed as long as we could. If we hadn't left, our asylum papers would not have been held for us. Then we would have been a family without a country to call home. We couldn't have returned to Afghanistan, and we couldn't have stayed in Pakistan."

"But she's out there all by herself," insisted Zafoona.

"Mother," whispered Noor, leaning across the aisle toward them. "Dad did what he could."

Zafoona's reddened eyes filled with tears, and she huddled in her woolen shawl.

"*Jaan*, your cousin Nargis has a crew of men in Peshawar looking for any news of Mariam," said Habib, rubbing Zafoona's hands to warm them. "Nargis said she'd call us first thing if she learns anything. And Professor Sahib is headed to Jalalabad with his sons to search along the Afghan border."

"But—," began Zafoona.

"Mother," Noor interrupted, "Mariam is an American citizen, so the U.S. consulate is keeping an eye out for her too. And I helped *Khala* Nargis post Mariam's pictures at the International Rescue Committee's office. If she comes over the border, they *will* find her."

"There are so many people looking for her, even your old schoolmate we ran into at the United Nations Refugee Agency's office," added Habib. "She will notify us if they or other local nongovernmental agencies dealing with displaced persons spot her."

Zafoona looked away from them and pursed her quivering lips. Noor settled back in her seat and sighed.

Fadi rolled the foil off his steaming chicken and, without much interest, removed the plastic silverware from its protective plastic bag. Watching the spoon slide into his hand, he paused, bewildered. Mariam's voice called out to him as if from a haze.

"Fadi!" shouted Mariam. "I want the spoon!"

"Oh, all right," grumbled Fadi, handing her the wooden spoon while he kept the steel fork with the crooked prong.

The sun was just about to set and the two of them were in the backyard, crouched under the lone plum tree. In less than twelve hours they would be in a taxi, headed toward Jalalabad. Fadi glanced back at the house as the last of the sun's rays glinted across the expanse of windows, tinting them silver. Withered rosebushes grew along the sides of the house, planted years ago by his grandfather. Fadi wondered if he'd ever see any of it again.

"Are you ready?" Mariam interrupted his morose thoughts, an eager smile playing on her lips.

"Yes, I'm ready," grumbled Fadi. He'd been cornered by her earlier that day, and in order to escape her chattering on and on about not leaving her treasure behind, he'd agreed to help.

For a moment Mariam's smile faltered as she looked around the base of the scraggly tree. She pooched out her cheeks and inspected the trunk, parched and peeling from the drought. Her eyes widened in alarm. "I don't remember where I buried it," she squeaked.

Fadi released a pent-up breath. "Mariam," he said quietly, "there's still packing to do, and we're leaving really early in the morning. Are you sure this treasure of yours is so important?"

"Yes," said Mariam, her lower lip trembling.

"Oh, all right. Don't cry," said Fadi. "Just pick a spot and start digging."

For the next hour, aided by the light of the full moon and a sputtering candle Fadi had found in the empty house, they crawled around in the dirt, excavating dozens of shallow holes. His fingernails caked in soil, Fadi was about to call it quits when the earth loosened around a small tin box in their twenty-sixth pit.

"There it is!" cried Mariam. Her small fingers pulled an old honey tin out from near the roots of the tree, and she sat back with a tremendous grin. Fadi could see the gleam of her teeth in the moonlight.

"Okay. What's in there that's so important?" he asked.

Mariam pulled open the rusty lid and shone the candle inside. Nestled in a scrap of purple velvet was a tiny jar of Mariam's baby teeth. Next to it was Gulmina's hand, which had been chopped off by the metal fence. There was a broken pearl earring that belonged to their mother, one of Noor's old belt buckles studded with gleaming colored glass, a shiny stone that resembled a gold nugget, her father's tassel from his graduation cap from the University of Wisconsin, and old water-stained pictures Fadi thought his mother had thrown out. One showed Fadi holding Mariam when she was a baby.

"Wow," said Fadi. "You saved all this stuff?"

"Yup," said Mariam. "It's all the memories of my life."

"Well, I'm glad we found it, then."

"Will you keep it in your backpack for me?"

"Absolutely," said Fadi, pulling Mariam up. Covered

in dust and clumps of dirt, they hurried inside to clean
up before their mother found them.

The spoon felt cold and clammy in his hands. Fadi
dropped it into his lap and leaned back from the tray
table. *There are a lot of people looking for her,* he thought.
She'll be found soon. But, niggled a dark voice in the back
of his mind, *she shouldn't have been lost in the first place. If
only I'd stopped to put her stupid doll in my backpack like she'd
asked me to, then she wouldn't have dropped it. It was all my
fault.* He pulled his bread roll apart, sending a shower of
crumbs over Noor.

"Watch it!" she growled.

He offered his slice of cake as a peace offering. She
took it and stabbed at it with her fork.

While in Pakistan he'd tried to sneak out of *Khala*
Nargis's house. He hadn't known exactly where he was
going, but he'd wanted to go look for Mariam. But
before he'd been able to exit the gates onto the chaotic
rain-drenched streets of Peshawar, Noor had caught
him.

"Where are you going?" she'd asked.

"Uh, to the corner store. To get some, uh, candy,"
he'd mumbled.

"You don't have any money." She'd stated the obvious.

"I was, uh . . ."

"Get back in the house," Noor had barked. "One missing kid is enough."

The piercing look she had given him had made Fadi wince. *She knows it's my fault Mariam got left behind.*

4 Arrival

WELCOME TO SAN FRANCISCO, announced the sign at the head of the cavernous international arrival hall. Fadi stood in the immigration line and looked around the sprawling airport in awe. Two other planes had arrived at the same time as their Virgin Atlantic flight, and the sea of pearly gray carpet swarmed with people, all waiting to have their papers processed.

"Move," ordered Noor. She pushed Fadi forward as their turn came.

"Papers, please," said the immigration officer. He wore a crisp white shirt with an official seal stitched on the right sleeve.

"Here you are," said Habib, handing him a large envelope. He gave Fadi a wink as the officer pulled out the pages.

"You're seeking asylum, I see?" the officer asked.

"Yes, sir."

Fadi looked at the thick pile of papers from the Consul General in Peshawar. It was the story of what had happened to them in Afghanistan and the danger Habib had faced when he'd been pressured to join the Taliban.

The officer entered a series of numbers into the computer, his face serious. After what seemed like an hour of typing, he turned his attention to the pile of passports.

"What's this?" he asked, pulling an American passport from the bundle. "There are four of you, so who is this fifth person? Mariam Nurzai?"

Fadi froze, watching Habib's fingers tighten around his fraying leather briefcase. His father had mistakenly handed over Mariam's paperwork along with theirs.

Noor's lips tightened into one of her perpetual frowns.

"She . . . she is our youngest daughter," said Habib, clearing his throat.

"Where is she?" asked the officer. He peered over the edge of the desk.

"She's not here," replied Habib. "She . . . she was accidentally left behind in Afghanistan."

"Accidentally left behind?" questioned the officer. His bushy blond eyebrows arched upward. He glanced over the rest of the family. His sharp blue eyes paused for a moment on Fadi, who looked down at his old tennis shoes.

"Yes. . . . It was an accident," said Habib. "But authorities are looking for her. . . . We hope to find her very soon," he added more forcefully.

The officer's gaze softened. "I have three daughters. Couldn't imagine one of them lost all alone like that." He nodded to Zafoona, who sat in a wheelchair provided by the airline, dabbing at her eyes. "God willing, she'll be found soon, ma'am." With that he stamped the family's passports with loud thumps and sent them on their way.

Fadi looked down the long hallway with bleary eyes. *Five years ago we were on our way back to Afghanistan from the United States. Mariam was a baby, barely able to walk.* A moment of anger flared through him. *It's Father's fault. We never should have gone back to Afghanistan in the first place when things were so bad.*

"Come along," said Habib, interrupting Fadi's thoughts.

They followed the signs directing them toward baggage claim. Once their small suitcases were collected from the luggage carousel, they proceeded through customs, had their luggage inspected, and then finally exited the wide double doors.

A sea of eager smiling faces bobbed around them, calling out names and waving cards with passenger's names on them.

"Who's coming to get us?" asked Noor, her face hidden behind a curtain of long, black hair.

"Your uncle Amin," said Zafoona. She leaned forward in her wheelchair to scan the crowd.

Fadi had vague memories of meeting Uncle Amin when they'd returned to Kabul five years before. Uncle Amin was married to Fadi's mother's younger sister, *Khala* Nilufer. Uncle Amin was his mother's third cousin or something, since Uncle Amin's mother was Zafoona's father's first cousin. Marriages in Afghan families could be complicated like that.

A jovial, smiling man, Uncle Amin had been a doctor at Kabul's main hospital. After it had been bombed during one of the many skirmishes between battling warlords, he had decided to leave the country. *Khala* Nilufer had repeatedly called Zafoona in Madison, urging them not to return to Kabul since they themselves were in the process of leaving. But Habib had been set on returning, convinced that refugees like

Amin and Nilufer would return once the Taliban brought law and order.

Within a month of Fadi's and his family's return, Uncle Amin had taken his family and his parents, Abay and Dada, across the border into Iran. For a year he'd worked in a refugee camp with an international aid organization. From there they'd gone to London, then to the United States. Zafoona's older brother also left Afghanistan for Germany later that year, along with his wife and children. Only Mastura, Zafoona's youngest sister, remained in Kabul. Her husband had been killed in the war with the Soviets, and she and her two children lived with her in-laws.

"There!" said Zafoona. "There he is!"

A tall balding man with an ample belly stood behind a woman carrying roses. He waved energetically at them.

"That's him," said Zafoona, a rare smile stretching her pale lips.

"*Salaam Alaikum!*" exclaimed Uncle Amin, giving Habib a hug. Behind him lurked a boy around Fadi's age, who leaned forward to give Zafoona a kiss on the cheek.

"*Mashallah*, Zalmay," said Zafoona. "You've gotten so tall and handsome."

Zalmay blushed and mumbled something,

"Fadi, come meet your cousin," said Zafoona.

"*Salaam Alaikum*," said Fadi. He reached out to shake Zalmay's hand.

"*Walaikum A'Salaam*," Zalmay responded. "You, uh, have a long trip?" he added in a rush.

"Yes." Fadi gave a weary grimace. "Really long."

"Zalmay, help your uncle Habib with the suitcases," said Uncle Amin. "Fadi, is that you? My goodness, you were a tiny fellow when I saw you back in Kabul. And, Noor, you have grown up into a young lady—no longer dashing around with pigtails and a runny nose."

Noor turned red and mumbled her *Salaam*s.

Fadi froze. *What if he asks about Mariam? Does he know?* Then he remembered. His parents had called Uncle Amin from Peshawar, as they had all their relatives, to tell them what had happened.

"Well, let's go," said Uncle Amin, leading them toward the wide glass doors that opened onto the curbside pickup area.

"Wait here and I'll bring the car around," said Uncle Amin.

Half an hour later Fadi was wedged firmly in the backseat of a beat-up Dodge Caravan. He dislodged Noor's elbow from his back and scooted closer to the door. He pressed his nose against the window, watching traffic as they exited the airport and merged onto Highway 101.

"So," said Habib, "how is the family doing?"

"All doing well, *Alhamdulillah*," said Uncle Amin. "Nilufer is so excited you are here. She and my mother have been cooking up a storm all day."

"Yes, yes," said Zafoona from the backseat. "It's been too long since I saw her. She was the best cook out of the three of us. I was always more interested in my studies."

"Well, you were first in your class, as I recall," said Uncle Amin, nodding. "Your parents were so proud when you were accepted to Kabul University. Especially your father, may Allah bless his soul."

"That seems like such a long time ago now," replied Zafoona with a deep sigh.

"How were things in Kabul when you left?" asked Uncle Amin. "We've heard that the drought this year was bad."

"Very bad," said Zafoona. "Low rainfall ruined this year's crops, and there have been food shortages. Many people have resorted to eating grass. Grass! Can you imagine?"

Uncle Amin shook his head sadly.

"The Taliban came with so much hope," said Habib, rubbing his red-rimmed eyes. "Now fighting with the Northern Alliance has flared up. They are all the same—power-hungry and arrogant."

"What is the problem with people?" said Uncle Amin, his grip on the steering wheel tightening. "What has happened to common decency?"

"War, war, always war," grumbled Zafoona. Fadi could see she was getting more exhausted by the discussion, and he squeezed her arm. He didn't want her to get breathless and succumb to a fit of coughing.

Zafoona glanced over at him with a smile and held his hand. She turned her attention back to the front.

"Maybe it's in our blood," said Uncle Amin with a shake of his head. "Afghanistan has been invaded so many times. By the Persians, Greeks, Arabs, Turks, Mongols, British, and then the Soviets . . ."

Fadi listened with half an ear. He'd heard it all before.

"But perhaps we are our own worst enemy," commented Habib quietly. "We are always fighting, either with others or among ourselves. No one has defeated the Afghans, but centuries of war have left our country full of strife—one of the poorest in the world."

As the adults continued their gloomy conversation and Zalmay played with a handheld video game, Fadi shrank back into the fading brown leather seat. He gazed in trepidation at the white-crested churning water of the San Francisco Bay as they headed across the San Mateo bridge. Fascinated, Fadi pressed his nose against the glass, feeling as if he could reach out with his hand and touch the cool water. A seagull flew low over the waves seemingly motionless, buffeted by the wind. The water below undulated in shades of blue to green to purple in some spots. Fadi thought of a book he'd read last year that he'd found at the underground book shop. *Twenty Thousand Leagues Under the Sea.* He wondered what kind of creatures lurked under the shifting water.

For a moment Fadi felt queasy, a little seasick. They were traveling awfully close to the water. Afghanistan was landlocked, with the nearest coast lying along the Arabian Sea three hundred miles to the south. Even when he was young, in Wisconsin, Fadi had never seen the ocean. This was the first time he'd been this close to so much water. A gazillion gallons of shimmering water flowed beneath them. *Mariam would have loved it.*

Reunion

WITH A BURP OF SMOKE BILLOWING FROM its tailpipe, the Dodge exited the bridge and hopped onto Interstate 880. They headed south for another ten miles, as a comfortable silence descended over them. Fadi looked at the cars racing by and marveled at their speed. He'd rarely left their house on Shogund Street these past few years. Although the Taliban had brought some order to the city, it still hadn't been safe to go outside. Zafoona had decided to homeschool Fadi, Noor, and Mariam, especially since all the girls' schools had been closed by the Taliban.

Fadi stared at the new white strands in his father's

hair and couldn't help but feel sorry for him. His father had wanted to go back to Afghanistan to help, but it just hadn't turned out that way. Initially he'd hoped to teach at the agriculture department at Kabul University. Founded in 1931, the university had once been the finest in Asia, the intellectual heart of the country. But after years of war it was in shambles and had to be shut down.

Habib had opened a small dry goods store in downtown Kabul to support the family after the opium crops had been destroyed. Every once in a while his father would take Fadi to work with him. Downtown Kabul's maze of streets was usually jam-packed with cars, donkey carts, and people on foot.

Fadi gazed out the window at the tall walls that lined either side of the freeway, sheltering buildings, shopping plazas, and parks on the other side. Everything looked so big and so new.

Uncle Amin eased his way into the right lane and took the Thornton Avenue exit into Fremont. They passed an elementary school and drove along a street lined with shops, teahouses, restaurants, and a small theater. Fadi rolled down the window to let in fresh air, and he caught a whiff of freshly baked bread. He could see signs in familiar Persian script on many of the storefronts.

"Here we are. Little Kabul—home away from the

real thing," joked Uncle Amin with a rumbling laugh.

"Really?" asked Habib, looking out the side window. A group of women in long dresses and head scarves strolled by.

"Fremont has the largest population of Afghans in the United States," said Uncle Amin. "There are dozens of Afghan restaurants, cafés, and shops. You can drop by, get a cup of tea, and hear the latest news."

"That must be nice," said Zafoona.

"Yes, it is. Nilufer can find all the ingredients she needs to make her famous kebobs and *pulaos*."

The mention of kebobs got Fadi's stomach rumbling. He hadn't eaten much on the plane and he was hungry.

"Ah, here we are," said Uncle Amin. He took a right turn down a residential street and pulled up next to a single-story brown shingle house with overgrown rose-bushes out front.

They had just stepped down out of the car when the front door burst open and a group of women and children came flying out.

"You're here!" cried a woman in a flowing dress. She looked like a younger version of Zafoona, but her hair was cut fashionably short and her eyes were leaf green.

"Nilufer," cried Zafoona, stumbling forward to give her sister an enveloping hug. Without warning they both burst into tears and started talking at once.

"Jeesh," said Zalmay. He exchanged an embarrassed look with Fadi, who grinned in return.

Behind Zafoona and Nilufer stood an elderly couple, who Fadi guessed were Abay, grandmother, and Dada, grandfather—Uncle Amin's parents.

Habib moved forward to kiss the old woman's cheeks. "*Salaam Alaikum*," he said reverently. "How good it is to see you."

"I'm so thankful to Allah you are here safely," she said, her voice as wispy as a spider's web. She kissed Habib's forehead and then his cheeks.

Cocooned in the flow of people, Fadi and his family were bundled into the house. Over the next half hour Fadi met a blur of people, which included Uncle Amin's two brothers and their wives and children. Zafoona was settled in a bedroom for a quick nap despite her protests that she wanted to help, while the other women retreated to the kitchen to prepare endless platters of food. The men caught up on the latest news, and the kids set out plates and cutlery.

"Let me say a prayer before we begin lunch," said Uncle Amin an hour later. The family sat around the traditional *dastarkhan*, a tablecloth laid out on the floor on top of which the food was placed. "Let us thank

Allah that Brother Habib and his family have made it safely to San Francisco."

As he paused, Fadi's back stiffened.

"May Allah also be watching over brave little Mariam, who, *insha*'Allah, will soon be found and brought here to us."

"There are dozens of people looking for her," said Habib. "She'll be found very soon."

Father's right. She'll be found soon, thought Fadi. *There are so many people looking for her.* The knot between his shoulder blades eased a bit.

"*Ameen,*" came the murmurs from around the room.

Fadi glanced at his mother. Tears pooled along her eyelashes. The familiar feeling of guilt returned, though he pushed it back. He looked around the room at the solemn faces. Even the younger kids were quiet. They must have been horrified at the thought of being lost out in the middle of nowhere. By themselves. *What if they knew it was my fault Mariam was lost? They'd hate me.*

Conversation buzzed around him, about their escape . . . about Mariam.

"Poor *bacha,*" came a whisper near his ear.

Startled, Fadi turned to see that Abay had settled down next to him. She placed a soft hand on Fadi's shoulder and pulled him in for a hug. Fadi stiffened, then melted into her embrace, which smelled of cardamom and cinnamon. He wondered if she could read the guilt in his face. He avoided her probing eyes and averted his face.

Abay patted him on the face and passed him a glass of fizzy orange drink. He gulped it down, the coolness easing the dryness in his throat. Steaming plates of food were passed around as Habib told them how, although neither the American consulate nor Nargis had tracked down Mariam yet, it was only a matter of time before she'd be found. The UN Refugee Agency had sent out a bulletin about Mariam, and Habib's professor and his sons were looking for any news of her in Jalalabad.

Khala Nilufer piled a mound of *qabuli pulau*—rice and lamb—onto Fadi's plate. He dug in, savoring the candied carrots and raisins. There was also spinach, fried eggplant with yogurt, and chicken stew. Abay added two *mantu* to his plate. Fadi stared down at the two plump dumplings smothered in a meat sauce, and his hunger vanished. *Mantu* was Mariam's favorite dish.

After lunch Fadi wandered toward the back of the small house, wanting to get away from the crush. Zalmay had offered to show him his collection of video games, but he wasn't interested. He ducked inside the empty kitchen.

The pantry door stood invitingly open, so he slipped inside. He slid to the ground between a huge bag of rice and shelves packed with canned goods and spices. He'd been sitting for a few solitary minutes when he heard footsteps enter through the doorway.

"So what *happened*, Zafoona?" prodded a concerned voice.

Fadi spotted *Khala* Nilufer through the gap between the door and the frame. He shrank into the shadow as chairs were pulled back from the small dinette set near the window.

"It's all a blur," said Zafoona, her voice scratchy. "We were at the appointed place when the truck arrived. It was late, well past midnight, and we hurried to get on board. Noor practically carried me because I was so sick. Habib led the way, carrying the suitcases, while Fadi and Mariam trailed behind. Then within seconds, complete chaos descended over us. . . . Dozens of people appeared from out of nowhere. There was a mad dash for the truck."

"Oh, my goodness," murmured *Khala* Nilufer.

"It's my fault she's lost, you know," whispered Zafoona.

Fadi stiffened. *Her fault?* He peered through the crack at his mother's hunched shoulders.

"Don't blame yourself, Zafoona *jaan!*" cried *Khala* Nilufer.

"She's *my* baby. I'm her mother. It's all *my* fault," cried Zafoona, and, she burst into ragged sobs.

Fadi could see her shoulders shaking as *Khala* Nilufer grabbed tissues. He closed his eyes, blocking out her tears, but he couldn't extinguish the anguished sounds.

"Zafoona," comforted *Khala* Nilufer, "you're making yourself sick. You can't think like this."

"No, you don't understand," said Zafoona. "If I wasn't so sick, I could have looked after her. But instead everyone was looking after *me*. Noor and Habib were so worried about getting me on board the truck that they lost track of Fadi and Mariam. It's my fault."

Fadi sank his fingernails into the bag of rice. *It wasn't her fault. She wasn't the one responsible for losing Mariam.*

"No, no, you can't think this way, Zafoona *jaan*," soothed Nilufer. "You were sick. You can't help that."

"I don't know . . ." Zafoona paused a few seconds. "I've always tried to be a good mother. But I've had to be the disciplinarian. Habib has always been the soft one, the one who the kids turn to when they skin their knees or want to share a secret. I hate to think that Mariam doesn't think I love or care for her."

"Of course Mariam knows you love her," said *Khala*

Nilufer forcefully. "You can tell her yourself when she comes home. There are so many people looking for her, she'll be found soon."

"*Insha'*Allah," said Zafoona softly.

"Now come and sit in the backyard," said *Khala* Nilufer. "The fresh air will do you good. I'll make a fresh pot of green tea."

As the women headed to the backyard with their tea, Fadi sat alone, in the dark. *It's where I deserve to be.*

6

Paradise

FADI TEETERED ON THE EDGE OF THE BED, inspecting the cramped room he and his family shared at the back of Uncle Amin's house. He glanced with unease at the calendar with the dancing cats. It was the last day of August 2001, and they'd been living there for more than six weeks. He twisted the silky bedspread in his fist as a sense of weary hopelessness settled over him.

Over the preceding weeks he'd sat, tucked away, next to the couch in the living room, listening while Habib and Uncle Amin called their relatives and friends in Afghanistan and Pakistan. Dozens of people were searching on both sides of the border, but without much success. Not even *Khala* Nargis's contacts had found any trace of a little girl named Mariam.

But would Mariam have told anyone her name? Fadi's chest tightened. He remembered his father ordering her never to reveal who she was. *Maybe they can't find her because they don't know who she is. How would she ever be found, then?*

At nine p.m. on Friday, as he did every week, Habib dialed the number given to him by the U.S. consulate in Peshawar, where it was nine in the morning, exactly twelve hours ahead. The week before, the scratchy voice of the assistant on the speakerphone had told them that she was still sending out inquiries, but the situation in Afghanistan was getting worse. The United Nations Security Council had passed a new resolution to tighten the monitoring and enforcement of sanctions against the Taliban. Because of this, things on the border had become very tense. Hopelessness threatened to turn to despair as Fadi remembered Mariam's tiny fingers slipping through his. *Father was so sure Mariam would be found in a few weeks.*

But week after week of no news, or bad news, had set Fadi's nerves on edge. He withdrew and kept to himself. Zalmay tried his best to pull Fadi out of his funk. He introduced him to his friends, dragged him to Lake Elizabeth park to feed the ducks, and let him play his best video games. After learning that Fadi liked taking photos, Zalmay even offered to pose for him, dressed as Superman, but Fadi's heart wasn't in it.

One day the entire family piled into two cars and headed to the Great Mall. It was the largest shopping complex in the Bay Area, built in an old Ford assembly plant. It was so different from the simple markets in Kabul that Fadi couldn't help but become distracted by the amazing array of stores, in particular the shop selling electronic gadgets. But when he later ran into Zafoona, wandering in a daze among rows of little girls' pink party dresses, he wanted to go home and hide in the kitchen pantry. After that the only thing he sort of wanted to do was sit with Abay, parked in front of the television. Her wrinkled face mirrored the emotions on the screen as he translated *ER, The Price Is Right,* and *Oprah* for her, which helped improve his English.

During the day when his mother was taking a nap and the other adults were at work, even Noor, who'd found a job at a nearby McDonald's, Fadi went online. He surfed the Web, looking for articles on Afghanistan and the flood of refugees pouring across the border. He kept typing in "Mariam Nurzai," hoping for a random hit. But there was nothing.

Fadi sighed, spotting the two suitcases standing at the foot of the bed. Everything was packed and ready to go, even the copy of *From the Mixed-up Files of Mrs. Basil E. Frankweiler.* He'd finally finished reading it but couldn't get himself to give the book away. It reminded him of Kabul, and for some odd reason, Claudia felt like a friend. She and her brother, while hiding at the Metropolitan Museum of Art, had managed to solve an amazing mystery concerning a Renaissance statue, and Fadi admired her guts. So he'd stuck the book into his backpack, and it had come to rest against the old honey tin. He couldn't get himself to take it out of the bag, so it just sat there.

Now we're moving out, thought Fadi, remembering the argument his parents had had with Uncle Amin and *Khala* Nilufer that morning.

"We can't keep living off of your hospitality," said Habib. He sat next to Zafoona at the kitchen table.

Fadi stood next to Zalmay in the hallway, listening in.

"Hospitality!" grumbled Uncle Amin. He looked a

bit insulted. "What are you talking about? My house is your house; my food is your food."

"Thank you for your kind words, Brother Amin," said Habib with a smile in his voice, "but we must move on."

"As a Pukhtun, I am insulted you are leaving my house," grumbled Uncle Amin.

"Habib, Brother Amin, stop arguing," said Zafoona. "This house is small as it is for your family. We have inconvenienced you enough."

"We're not inconvenienced," said *Khala* Nilufer. She placed her hands on her sister's shoulders, as if trying to keep her from leaving.

Fadi knew otherwise. After immigrating to the United States three years ago, Uncle Amin hadn't passed the medical board exams needed to practice as a doctor. So he worked two jobs as a lab technician at the morgue to support the family, while still studying when he had time. Then, two weeks ago, Uncle Amin's brother had lost his job and had moved into the house with his wife and three children. During the day the line for the bathroom sometimes stretched down the hall. Now the adults seemed to talk a lot about some kind of recession thing that was going on.

"You are family," stressed Uncle Amin. "You need to

get back on your feet, and then you can leave."

"I'm earning a decent living driving a taxi," said Habib.

Fadi winced. His father had hoped to teach at the local community college, but there just wasn't an opening in the agriculture department.

"But what about Zafoona?" pushed *Khala* Nilufer. "The doctors still don't know what's wrong with her. She needs to be taken care of."

"It's all right, Nilufer *jaan*," interrupted Zafoona. "I'm feeling much better. Noor and Fadi can help me. We're only moving a few blocks away, so you can visit me anytime you want."

"I'm coming to pick you up for your doctor's appointment next week," insisted *Khala* Nilufer. "You're not getting out of that."

"Of course," said Zafoona.

After some more grumbling it was decided. They were moving out on their own.

There was nothing heavenly about the place Fadi's father had rented at the Paradise Apartment Complex. They could only afford a cramped two-bedroom unit with faded linoleum, brown shag carpet, and a cracked kitchen sink. Fadi stood at the entrance and sighed. It was a stiflingly hot August day, and the apartment, a tenth the size of their house on Shogund Street, was sweltering. As Fadi explored the cramped space, he felt a sense of claustrophobia. There was no beauty here, just the faded ghosts of past tenants who'd moved on to better things. Noor had grumbled at the idea of sharing a bedroom with him, so he'd happily given it up, deciding it was better to sleep on the floor in the living room.

That first night in the apartment, Fadi lay on the living room floor, cocooned in a bedroll made up of old blankets from the Salvation Army. His mother had gone to bed early, and both Habib and Noor were at work. Fadi lay wide awake, a faded Batman comforter pulled up to his chin. He didn't want to look up at the ugly web of cracks across the ceiling. It made him think of a large, poisonous spider that was out to catch him. He punched the lumpy pillow and flipped to his other side, but sleep continued to evade him. He sat up and pulled the copy of *From the Mixed-up Files of Mrs. Basil E. Frankweiler* from his backpack. Fadi crept over to the open window and settled under a cool incoming breeze. In the soft light of the full moon, he cracked open the dog-eared book to one of his favorite parts.

He had to admit that Claudia was one smart girl. She'd really planned out her escape to the Metropolitan Museum of Art with great precision. She'd even talked her brother into coming along; he was a miser and had a lot of money. Fadi was wondering what she would have done if she had gotten caught, when he heard a key rattle in the front door. Fadi slipped the book under the sofa and dove under the covers, pretending to be asleep.

"Thanks for picking me up, Father," came Noor's tired voice.

"I insist on it, *jaan*," came Habib's answer. "This late at night I don't want you walking home alone."

"All right."

There was the sound of a zipper sliding open.

"Father, I want to give you this," whispered Noor.

There was a silence as Fadi strained his ears. *What is Noor giving Father?*

"Father, are you all right?"

After a brief silence Habib responded. "This is your money, Noor *jaan*. You've earned it, and I'm very proud of you."

"Father, I'd like to give you part of it to . . . to help out. I know money is tight," she added.

"You're the most excellent of daughters," whispered

Habib, his voice tight with emotion. "And your money will be of great help to the family."

Fadi couldn't believe it. Noor was giving Father money she'd earned at McDonald's?

"Now come, let's eat some of that beef stew your *khala* Nilufer dropped off earlier. I'm famished from all that driving. Some crazy woman had me go around the city for hours looking for a hat shop that didn't exist. At least I earned quite a bit on that ride."

"Father," said Noor, her voice dropping an octave, "I have to tell you something. Something I've been meaning to tell you . . . but not in front of Mother."

Fadi stiffened. His mind raced with terrible thoughts. *She knows!*

"What is it?"

"That day in Jalalabad . . . the day we left Afghanistan . . ." Noor's voice tightened.

"Yes, what about that day?"

Fadi lay in his bedroll. Sweat began to accumulate under his armpits. *She's going to tell him . . . tell him I lost Mariam . . .*

"I let you down," whispered Noor.

"Let me down? What are you talking about?"

"I was supposed to take care of Fadi and Mariam. But in all the confusion . . . I left them behind."

"No, *jaan*, you did nothing wrong," soothed Habib.

"No, I'm the oldest. I should have taken care of them. . . . It's my fault Mariam is lost!"

Fadi went rigid with shock. He couldn't believe Noor thought it was her fault that Mariam had been lost.

Everyone thinks it's their fault she's gone. But it's my fault, not anyone else's. I'm the one who doesn't deserve to belong to this family. I'm the one who's torn it apart.

Brookhaven

FADI WATCHED NOOR CLOSELY THE ENTIRE weekend before school started. He observed her fingers, tipped with black nail polish, turn the pages of the book she was reading as she lounged on the fraying orange sofa. He stood at the sink washing dishes as she spread peanut butter on saltine crackers. He spied around the corner while she carried a bowl of steaming soup for their mother. The more he watched, the more he realized that Noor no longer seemed angry or aloof. She appeared preoccupied . . . and sad. He realized that he'd been so caught up with his own worries that he hadn't thought about what she had been going through the past few months.

Noor had recently cut off her long dark hair, revealing delicate features and making her dark brooding eyes more pronounced. Their mother had been disappointed when she'd seen it and had told her so, but Noor had told her that it was hot standing next to the McDonald's French-fryer all day long, and short hair was much cooler. Fadi thought the new style looked nice on her but hadn't had the nerve to tell her.

He wished he could talk to Noor. More than half a dozen times he'd resolved to tell her that it wasn't her fault Mariam had been left behind. It was his fault. Finally, on Sunday evening he took a pile of laundry to her room and stood at the door, tongue-tied. She pointed to her bed and ignored him as she ironed her shirts. He looked at her profile, his tongue clamped between his teeth. As she opened her mouth to say something, he dumped the clothes onto the bedspread and ran out. He couldn't do it. If he told her it wasn't her fault, he'd have to admit that it was his, and he didn't have the guts to say it out loud.

On Tuesday morning Habib drove the short distance from their apartment to Brookhaven Middle School. Zafoona had surprised them by getting up early that morning and making them breakfast—Fadi's favorite of a fried egg and peanut butter on toasted Afghan bread. Fadi sat in the front seat, envying Noor, who didn't start high school till later that week. As his father filled out the registration paperwork in the school office, Fadi gazed out the window at the students filing into the adjacent elementary school. A girl with a long plait down her back caught his eye. Her bouncy walk reminded him of Mariam.

Mariam should have been starting the first grade, he thought, and his spirits sank lower. He wished his mother were well enough to homeschool him, like she used to—but that was not a possibility.

The school secretary's sharp voice snapped him out of his morose thoughts.

"Welcome to Brookhaven, young man," she said. She peered down at him through bifocal glasses and handed him a hard plastic debit card. "This card gets you a free lunch, so present it to the cashier in the cafeteria after you get your food."

"Thank you," said Fadi. As he slipped the card into his backpack, he saw the tight expression on his father's face.

"Thank you," said Habib with a nod to the secretary. "I forgot to pack him a lunch today, so this is great."

It's because we're poor, realized Fadi as a sense of unease settled over him. *That's why I get a free lunch.*

"Have a great day, Fadi," said Habib. "I want to hear all about it when you get home." After a quick hug Habib hurried back out to his taxi. He had to report to the airport for work, and he didn't want to be late. His dispatcher was already upset with him since he didn't know his way around the Bay Area that well yet. A taxi driver who couldn't take his passenger to the right address didn't make a lot of money.

With his class schedule clenched in his hand, Fadi stood in the doorway leading out of the office. He stared down the long hallway packed with kids and tried to get his bearings. A stream of students walked by, greeting old friends, high-fiving one another. *There's so many of them.* He was used to being in a room with just his sisters while Zafoona homeschooled them individually. The egg and peanut butter in his stomach gurgled unpleasantly, making him queasy.

"Anything wrong, honey?" the secretary asked from her desk.

"Uh, no," said Fadi in a hoarse whisper. Bracing himself, he followed the directions on the map to his homeroom, weaving through a sea of students. He walked through the unfamiliar halls, passing groups of girls and boys clustered together, joking, laughing—looking like they belonged. Fadi felt like an unnoticed shadow no one cared about. The only person he knew wasn't even in the same building. Just a year behind Fadi, Zalmay attended the elementary school next door. They'd spoken the night before and had agreed to meet after school, but it wasn't the same.

Fadi paused at the intersection of two halls and waited for a group of guys in sport jerseys to walk by. A girl sat at a small desk at the junction, handing out flyers. The sign she'd taped to the front read ANH FOR CLASS PRESIDENT! Most people ignored her, while some took the flyers only to dump them into the trash farther down the hall. Still the girl persisted, her face set with determination.

Fadi walked past the bathrooms, and finally he reached room 145. With a deep breath he turned the knob and entered. Loud laughter and shouts greeted him. Kids were hanging out talking, throwing wads of paper at one another. With a sinking feeling he noted that most of the desks were taken, except for the ones in front. *I definitely don't want to sit there.*

As curious glances fell his way, he spotted an empty spot on the other side of the room, in the middle of the row. His head ducked down, Fadi hurried across the room and slid into the seat with a feeling of some relief. He put his backpack under his desk and smoothed out his schedule on the scarred desktop. Ignoring the surrounding cacophony, he noted that math was next. *Okay. Math is good and pretty easy.* It was followed by science, then lunch. Language arts and physical education rounded out the rest of the day. His heart quickened when he saw he had art later on that week, on Thursday.

As he folded his page and slipped it into his bag, two boys in the back launched paper airplanes at the girls in the second row. It hit the head of a girl with sparkling pink barrettes in her pale yellow hair. With flushed plump cheeks she twisted around in her seat.

"Stop that, Ike!" she yelled. She crumpled up the plane and threw it back at a wiry red-haired boy, who Fadi guessed was Ike.

"What you going to do about it, Fatty Patty?" mocked Ike.

"Yeah, Fatty," echoed Ike's dark-featured friend, his lips curved with laughter. "What you gonna do? Eat us?"

"Good one, Felix," said Ike, giving him a high five.

Felix pretended to run his hands through his black spiky gelled hair and leaned back in his seat.

Patty turned red, sniffed, and turned around.

"Ignore them, Patty," consoled her friend, shooting

the boys a peeved look. "They're such morons. Have been since kindergarten."

Wow. These kids have known each other forever, thought Fadi in wonder.

Ike was about to say something in response when the door flew open. A man in a bright yellow-and-purple striped shirt hurried in and closed the door behind him. His hair, slightly past his shoulders, looked like it hadn't been combed in a very long time. "Sorry I'm late, class," he said. "Traffic got the best of me today. I promise it'll be the last time—so don't tell the principal."

Giggles followed his last remark as he picked up a piece of chalk. His arm, along with the rest of his body, flew across the board as he wrote his name.

"I'm Mr. Torres, your homeroom teacher for 6B. I'll also be teaching World History and Civilizations. So if you're not supposed to be in 6B, you're in the wrong room."

Kids looked around the room, to see if anyone got up to leave.

Fadi peeked at his schedule to double-check. *Yup, this is where I'm supposed to be.* There was no need for an embarrassing walk to the correct classroom.

"Well, looks like I've got a smart bunch this year," said Mr. Torres with a grin. He reached into his bag

and removed a sheaf of papers. "Here are the announcements for this week and the lunch menu."

Fadi's mind drifted off as Mr. Torres's words floated
over him. He gazed out the window, watching squir-
rels scamper down the trees, hiding nuts in the lawn.
He closed his left eye and fit the bushy-tailed creature
into a frame. *That would make a great picture,* he thought,
wishing he was outside with them.

Fadi added a few finishing touches to his drawings
of amoebas and other single-celled micro-organisms,
which the class had been reviewing. He slowly slipped
the pages into his science notebook and waited for the
rest of the kids to rush out to lunch. He hadn't said a
single word to anyone since homeroom that morning,
and no one had made the effort to talk to him, either.
He'd spotted two Afghan kids whispering to each other
in Farsi in math class, but he couldn't get himself to
walk up to them. *It's as if I don't exist.* At least the class-
work didn't look too hard. They were doing fractions
in math, which he'd covered with his mother last year.

Fadi put on his backpack, glanced at the school map
on the back of his schedule, and headed toward the cafeteria. With only one wrong turn that had him double

back, he found the beige double doors to the lunch-room. He paused for a moment and dug into the side pocket of his backpack for his lunch card. With the hard plastic rectangle hidden in his palm, he walked into the noisy sprawling space. He spotted the two Afghan kids from his math class and followed them from a distance. He grabbed a tray and got in line. The kids around him were telling one another about all the fun stuff they'd done that summer—trips to Disneyland, camping in Yosemite National Park, or swimming at the beach.

Fadi looked at them in growing annoyance. *I bet none of them ran away and lost their kid sister in the process.*

"What would you like?" asked the tired-looking woman behind the counter.

Fadi looked at his budgeted options—cheeseburger minis with French fries or something called a "bean and cheese burrito." The cheeseburgers he recognized. The burrito thing looked funny to him. He was still getting used to American food, and he wasn't sure he liked a lot of it yet. Peanut butter he liked. He could eat it every day, spread over Afghan bread, with plum jam.

"Hurry up," grumbled a voice behind him.

Fadi glanced back and froze. It was the kid from homeroom. The tall one with narrow almond-shaped eyes. *Ike's friend. What was his name? Felix.*

Felix's eyes narrowed. "What are you staring at?"

"Nothing," whispered Fadi. He averted his gaze down to Felix's flashy high-top sneakers and looked away.

"I haven't got all day," said the woman. She adjusted her hairnet and tapped her spoon against the glass case, pointing down.

"Those, please," said Fadi, pointing to the steaming tray of burgers. In a rush he added a carton of apple juice and hurried toward the cash register.

Before the cashier could say anything, Fadi quickly handed him the plastic card. He looked back at Felix, who, thankfully, was still deciding what he wanted. The cashier slid the card through the register and got a loud beep.

"When did you get this?" he asked. He pulled out the card and inspected it over the rim of his glasses.

"Uh, this morning."

The man rang up the purchase again and got another loud beep. "Hold on. I need to call the office."

"Try it again, please," pleaded Fadi. *Come on, come on, work,* he prayed, glancing back at Felix, who was getting a giant Coke to go with his slice of pizza from the concession stand.

The cashier entered the numbers one more time as

Fadi held his breath. The machine accepted the purchase and spit out a receipt. "Well, what do you know," the cashier said.

Just as Felix plunked his tray down next to Fadi's, the cashier handed back the card.

Fadi pocketed it quickly and moved on with his tray, but he caught Felix's smirk as the other boy took out his money and handed it to the cashier. His stomach sank. *This isn't good.*

The cafeteria was practically bursting at the seams. Students packed the benches, sharing stories and eating lunch. Fadi stood at the side, looking over the sea of unfamiliar faces, wondering where to sit. He cursed, wishing Zalmay had the same lunch period as him. Not finding an empty table, he walked to the back and sat on the ground next to the emergency exit. He took his apple juice and opened it as a girl with long black hair walked by. She was so busy talking to her friends that she didn't notice that her wallet had dropped out of her tiny pink purse. Fadi picked it up and followed her.

"Excuse me," he said, "I think this is yours."

The girl's almond-shaped eyes widened in surprise. "Thanks. That's really decent of you."

Fadi recognized her. She was the one running for

class president. "No problem," he said with a shrug.

"My name's Anh, Anh Hong." She stuck out her hand with authority.

Fadi gave her a weak shake. "I'm Fadi. Fadi Nurzai."

"Well, thanks again, Fadi," Anh said. She moved on with her friends.

Taking a bite of his cheeseburger, Fadi sat alone, watching students flurry around him like snowflakes in a blizzard. He felt as though he were hidden behind a camera lens, watching another world whirl past in shattered fragments.

8
Spotted

MUFFLED VOICES ECHOED down the hallway as Fadi came up the stairs to the family's apartment. *No one's supposed to be home,* he thought, pressing his ear against the front door. He could hear Uncle Amin's voice rumbling inside. Fadi inserted his key and pushed open the door to find his parents, Uncle Amin, and *Khala* Nilufer in the living room, huddled around a pot of tea and sugared almonds.

"Professor Sahib found a group of women who were trying to get on the truck that night," Habib explained to the other adults. "They remembered seeing a little girl standing on the side of the road, crying." His face was flushed as he looked up to see Fadi enter.

Fadi's heart pounded as he retreated around the corner into the hall. He didn't want to be told to go out to play or something. He wanted to hear what was going on.

Habib continued. "They were a group of sisters taking their father to Peshawar for medical treatment. They were having a difficult time with the old man because he was so sick."

I remember them, thought Fadi, his heart pounding. He'd stepped over the poor old man in his rush to get to the truck.

"Well," continued Habib, "the women said the crowd dispersed within seconds as the Taliban came roaring down the road, in pursuit of the truck. The women picked up their father and hid in one of the warehouses."

"Are they sure it was Mariam?" asked *Khala* Nilufer.

"Their description matches Mariam's features and what she was wearing," said Habib.

"Did they see what happened to her?" pressed Zafoona.

"One of the sisters, Aisha, the one Professor Sahib spoke to, felt bad that a little girl was out there all alone, so she came out to look for her."

"Oh, Allah, have mercy," said Uncle Amin.

"Aisha spotted Mariam talking to a family and

thought she'd been found by her parents . . . so she went back into the warehouse."

"Family? What family?" whispered Zafoona.

"A man, his wife, and two sons," said Habib. "That's who Aisha remembers seeing before she returned to the warehouse. Professor Sahib found another man who'd been unable to get onto the truck that night, but the man didn't remember seeing Mariam or the family Aisha was talking about."

"Who knows what kind of people she's with," moaned Zafoona.

"They must be good people," soothed *Khala* Nilufer. "They took in a helpless little girl."

"But who knows where they took her!" cried Zafoona.

"Well, we know the family was trying to get to Peshawar," said Uncle Amin logically. "They'll probably get the traffickers to bring them over the border since their passage has been paid for. Once Mariam reaches Peshawar, it will be much easier to find her."

"Habib told Mariam not to tell anyone who she is," interrupted Zafoona. "What if she doesn't tell these people her real name? She'll tell them she's the daughter of a simple farmer or goat herder, or something else."

She's right, thought Fadi, sweat beading on his forehead. *Father had told her not to tell anyone who she was.*

"We have to go back to Peshawar," said Zafoona, sounding more desperate by the minute. "We shouldn't have come here without finding her first."

"We couldn't do that," said Habib softly. "We would have been stuck in Pakistan without the chance for asylum. We would be a family without a country. There was no way we could go back to Afghanistan."

"What's more important? Gaining asylum or finding our daughter?" shouted Zafoona. "If it wasn't for your stubborn insistence that we go back to Afghanistan five years ago, we wouldn't be in this mess right now!"

Fadi's knees shook as he leaned against the wall. He'd never heard his mother speak to his father like this.

"Where is your *ghayrat*?" said Zafoona, her voice bitter.

A hush fell over the apartment as Fadi froze. Questioning a man's *ghayrat*, or ability to uphold his family's honor, was one of the most insulting things you could say to a Pukhtun. Fadi knew his father had to be furious, and embarrassed in front of the others.

"Now, Zafoona *jaan*, don't blame Brother Habib," said *Khala* Nilufer in a rush. "Who was to know this would happen? It was an accident. It's no one's fault."

"Oh, Habib," sobbed Zafoona, her mood mercurial. "I'm so sorry. I shouldn't have said that. . . . It's just that I'm so tired, and the medicines, they make my head swim. . . . I'm just not myself these days."

"No," came Habib's quiet voice. "You're right. It is my fault. I am head of this family. It was my responsibility."

Silence descended over the apartment. Fadi sank to his knees, overwhelmed with guilt. It was his fault that Mariam had been left behind, not his father's, not Noor's, not his mother's. He inched back toward the living room and came to a halt in front of the group. He gulped, opening his mouth to confess. But as the words formulated in his brain, something else flew out entirely.

"Mariam knows where we were going," blurted Fadi. "I told her about Mother's cousin who lives in Peshawar and that she was going to meet us at the border."

"You told her that?" said Zafoona, wiping away tears.

"Yes," said Fadi, "but I didn't remember *Khala* Nargis's name, just that she was your cousin and that she and her husband ran a clinic for refugees."

"So she knows we have family in Peshawar," said *Khala* Nilufer, her face eager. "That's good. Maybe she'll tell the family she's with to take her to a clinic."

"Allah willing, maybe she'll find us!" said Zafoona, a spark of light entering her eyes.

"Good job, Fadi," said Uncle Amin. "You should have told us this a long time ago."

"It's a good possibility," said Habib, holding up his hand, "but let's not get our hopes up too much."

"Then find the money to go back to Peshawar, Habib," said Zafoona. She shot her husband an angry look. "Let's go to the border and find her."

Habib closed his eyes and looked the other way. "I would love to do that, *jaan*," he whispered. "But you know as well as I do, that will take time."

Fadi looked at the sadness on his father's face and wanted to hide away in a ball of shame. *It's me that has no honor. All this is my fault. I have to do something. But what?*

After a quick snack of crackers and peanut butter, Fadi grabbed his camera and left the apartment. Noor had returned from work, and their parents were telling her about Professor Sahib's phone call. He caught a glimpse of hope on her face just as the door closed behind him. He clambered down the stairs and exited the apartment complex. It was a warm September day, and it felt good to have the sun shining on his back as he walked along Paseo Padre Parkway, heading toward Lake Elizabeth park.

Mother was right about one thing, he thought morosely. *If only we had enough money to go back to look for Mariam. I bet she's gotten across the border. She's looking for us, I just know it.*

But where would the money come from? It cost thousands of dollars, and his father barely made enough to pay for rent and food. Even with Noor's help, there was no way they could collect that much. *Maybe I can get a job. But where?* You had to be fifteen to work. Maybe he could get a paper route like Zalmay's friend. But that would take years to save up.

He needed a younger brother like Claudia's, who had a ton of money, or he needed to have a stroke of good luck. Claudia and her brother had hit the jackpot while hiding out at the Metropolitan Museum of Art. Claudia, a stickler for cleanliness, had insisted that she and her brother take a bath in the museum's fountain late at night. While wading through the water, they'd found heaps of coins lying on the tiled bottom. Over the years visitors to the museum had thrown money into the fountain for good luck. Claudia and her brother had ended up using the fountain as their own private piggy bank. But Fadi didn't have a loaded sibling or access to such a bank. He kicked a pebble on the sidewalk in frustration and stubbed his toe.

"Ow!" he grumbled.

Maybe I can borrow the money from someone. But who? Uncle Amin wasn't a possibility. He didn't make a lot of money, and he was supporting his brother, who was out of work. Then again, his father would have borrowed money from someone, if it had been a possibility, and returned to Pakistan to look for Mariam.

Professor Sahib's news, along with all this thinking, was giving Fadi a headache. He rubbed his forehead with his fingers and waited at the crosswalk. As the little man on the light changed to white, he followed a woman pushing a stroller to the other side of the street. The sound of music floated through the air as an ice cream truck came around the corner.

It's Mr. Singh, remembered Fadi, *Uncle Amin's neighbor across the street.* When he'd first met Mr. Singh the week of his arrival, he'd been surprised to see that the jovial ice cream truck driver had a beard and turban, similar to many Afghans. But he wasn't Afghan, or even Muslim. He was from India, and his beard and turban were signs of his Sikh religious beliefs.

Mr. Singh always gave the kids a discount when *Khala* Nilufer got them Popsicles. Man, Popsicles . . . a genius American invention. That and Twinkies, peanut butter, lime Jell-O and Snickers bars. He looked with a frown at the group of kids gathering around the small white truck. *Darn. I wish I had some money. But I don't even have a dime to my name.* He was about to trudge on when a familiar flash of red caught his eye. It was Ike and his buddy!

Fadi dove behind a tree just as Felix ran over, carrying two large ice cream cones. Fadi stood watching them, hoping they weren't hanging out in the park. The boys were standing on the corner, licking their cones, when a sleek gray Mercedes–Benz pulled up next to them. Even though it was a red zone, the car stopped, and a dark-haired woman in a tailored black suit popped out. Felix stiffened and threw his cone into the bushes. The woman waved her finger at Felix and pointed back to her watch. Her hair swung angrily as she gestured to the car and climbed back in. His jaw clenched, Felix nodded to Ike and got into the passenger seat. As the car took off in a squeal of tires, Ike headed toward the bus stop.

Good, thought Fadi with relief. *They're gone.*

By the time Fadi made it over to the edge of the lake, the sun had begun to sink into the line of clouds on the horizon. Hints of pink, lavender, and gray appeared at the tops of the trees. Fadi took his camera from his backpack and removed the lens cap. This was the first time in months that he'd had a chance to use it. He looked through the viewfinder and aimed it toward the golden hills in the distance. A sense of calm flowed through him as he went through the familiar motions of framing different shots.

Fadi turned the ring on the lens and focused on a family of ducklings swimming on the glistening water. He framed the last little duckling in the viewfinder and clicked. He clicked again as a little boy was yanked from the edge of the lake by his distracted mother. The look on the kid's face was priceless—outrage mixed with relief. Fadi looked toward the grass and caught the image of a dog running after a Frisbee. A tall ebony-skinned woman in a lime green jumpsuit ran by him, and he caught her tennis shoes in motion.

"Hi," she called out, flashing a smile.

Fadi blushed and pointed his camera somewhere else.

Soon he was lost in capturing images of carefree children playing on the jungle gym or pumping their legs on the swings. There was no film in the camera, but that didn't matter.

After his father had given him the camera, he'd taught Fadi how to use it, sharing his own passion for photography. They used to go up into the hills in Kabul and take pictures of the city below them. Habib had

had a small darkroom set up in their house on Shogund Street, and when he could get his hands on supplies, they would develop the rolls they had taken together. But as the Taliban had gained more power, they had banned photography, so that had ended their forays outside. When his father had brought home the news of the photography ban, his cheeks had flushed with anger. "These are not true Muslims," he'd grumbled. "In Islam there is no compulsion in religion. One person does not have the right to dictate how another believes or lives."

Fadi sighed, wishing his father were with him, but these days Habib was too busy, or too tired, to waste time clicking away with a camera. His headache gone, Fadi went back to brainstorming about how to get enough money to fly back to Pakistan. *I got into this mess. I need to figure out how to get out of it.*

9
Colors

IT WAS THURSDAY, third period, and for the first
time in a long while Fadi felt a sense of eager anticipa-
tion buzz through his body. As soon as the bell rang,
he left Mr. Torres's World History and Civilizations
class and wove his way through the crowds to reach
the large studio at the back of the school. He paused
at the doorway—the smell of paint, plaster, and glue
permeated the air. Bright paintings and drawings decorated the walls, and clay sculptures stood along the
back of the room. Art supplies sat in organized piles on
tall shelves—paint, colored pencils, construction paper,
glue, and a myriad of other things he didn't recognize

but couldn't wait to inspect. Taking a deep sniff, Fadi entered, strolling past the tables placed in a circle in the center of the room. His fingers trailed along the paint-spattered surface as he looked for a spot that suited him.

As he chose a seat facing the front, he noticed a familiar face at the door. The girl tossed her black hair over her shoulder and gave him a wave. It was Anh from the cafeteria. Fadi responded with a tentative nod and looked away. *She's just being nice because I returned her wallet.* He sat down and turned his attention to a collection of black-and-white photographs tacked onto a corkboard. *Cool.*

A tall black woman in a shimmering silver top stepped out from one of the supply closets. "Attention, class," she called out. She strode to the middle of the room and motioned for everyone to take a seat. Her bracelets jingled as the kids stopped chitchatting and took their seats.

She looks familiar, thought Fadi. The memory of where he'd seen her was there, on the tip of his mind, but someone sat down next to him and interrupted his train of thought.

It was Anh. She pulled out a pad of paper and a pencil. "Hey, Fadi, how are you doing?"

Fadi blinked in surprise. "Uh, good."

"Do you like art?"

Before Fadi could answer, she continued, "This is a really fun class. I always choose it as my elective."

"Quiet down, class," ordered the teacher. "Most of you have taken art with me for the last few years, but for new students, my name is Ms. Bethune. Welcome, all of you. I hope you had a great summer. This year we're going to focus on color and contrast, and our first project is going to be done in a group. So I need you all to get into groups of threes."

Fadi's stomach sank as kids called out to their friends, breaking out into groups. He was going to be left out. He didn't know anyone.

"So, do you want to be in my group?" asked Anh.

Fadi blinked. "Really? You want me?"

"Yeah," said Anh. "I always like working with different people. It makes things more interesting."

As the groups finished assembling, one last boy stood standing. Fadi recognized him from math class and felt sorry for him; his light brown hair stood in a halo on top of his head while large glasses magnified his watery blue eyes, making him look like a confused owl chick.

"Let's ask him," said Fadi.

"Sure," said Anh, waving at the boy to join them.

The boy pointed at himself and mouthed, "Who? Me?"

Fadi nodded.

With a wide, relieved smile the boy hurried over to their table and introduced himself as Jonathan Greenly, Jon for short.

The three of them huddled together as Ms. Bethune gave instructions on what to do, then left them alone to brainstorm.

"Look, I don't know much about art," said Jon. He pushed his glasses up on his nose. "Everything I draw looks like a stick figure."

"Well, we need to come up with a theme," said Anh. She pulled a large yellow notepad from her bag.

Fadi and Jon nodded in agreement.

"How about the forest?" said Anh.

"Ooh," said Jon, scratching a red rash on his arm. "I got poison ivy while camping last week."

"That looks painful," said Fadi. "Does it hurt?"

"Nah, it just itches," said Jon, giving his arm another good scratch.

Anh frowned as another thought distilled in her mind. "How about the sky?"

Jon looked unconvinced.

"How about something from the movies? Or books?" she said, hoping inspiration would strike.

Jon perked up. "Movies, huh?"

"Well yeah," said Anh. "Classics like *Gone with the Wind* or *Casablanca*."

Jon wrinkled his nose. "Aren't those in black and white? I don't watch those."

Fadi hadn't heard of either one, but kept his mouth shut.

"What do you watch?" asked Anh.

"Well, I like scary movies, like *Friday the 13th*, or anything with Arnold Schwarzenegger in it, like *The Terminator* or *Predator*."

Anh rolled her eyes and wrote "scary movies" on her pad of paper.

"The sea," said Fadi under his breath.

"The what?" said Jon.

"The sea. Like in the book *Twenty Thousand Leagues Under the Sea*."

"Oh, yeah," said Jon. "I've seen that movie."

"It's also a book," said Anh with a grin. "And that's a totally cool idea! We could do the colors of the ocean and all the different creatures that live there!"

Fadi smiled as Anh's pen flew across the lined page.

As the class wrapped up, Ms. Bethune held up her hand for people to quiet down. "Class, just one announcement before the bell. The photo club will be holding its first official meeting next week on Tuesday, here in the art studio. You need to have access to a 35 millimeter SLR film camera. If you're interested, the sign-up sheet is on my desk. I'm holding an informal meeting to discuss plans for this year's club after school today."

Fadi's heart raced. *A photo club!* But Ms. Bethune's next sentence hit him like a bucket of cold water.

"The fee for supplies and use of the darkroom is fifty dollars, which can be paid in cash or your parents can write me a check."

There was no way he could come up with that much money.

"Are you going to join?" asked Anh.

Jon shook his head while Fadi shrugged without commitment.

"You should. I was in it last year, and it's a lot of fun. We have a few great photographers come in for special lessons, and we go all over the city for photo shoots," said Anh.

At the end of class Fadi passed by Ms. Bethune's desk. "Great theme, Fadi," she said. "The sea is going to give a lot of scope to be very creative."

"Thanks," said Fadi, eyeing the photo club sign-up sheet.

"Do you want to join?"

Fadi paused, conflicting desires racing through him.

"You seem to know what to do with a camera," she said, causing Fadi to look at her in surprise.

"It was you at Lake Elizabeth, right?" asked Ms. Bethune, giving him a closer look.

Then Fadi remembered the woman in cool red tennis shoes. It had been Ms. Bethune.

"I like taking pictures," he said lamely.

"Well, sign up, then," she urged with a smile.

Fadi grabbed the pen and wrote down his name. With a heavy heart he exited the studio.

Walking home from school, Fadi passed the McDonald's where Noor worked. He'd never had the nerve to go see her, but today, for some reason, maybe because he didn't want to go back to an empty apartment, he went inside. The pungent scent of hot oil hit him as he stopped near the counter. She wasn't at the register. He peered behind the milk shake machine, down the narrow galley. She wasn't at her post at the french-fryer either. *She probably left.* He exited the store and circled around back, taking a shortcut to get back to the apartment complex.

As he rounded the corner, the sound of muffled laughter filtered out from near the Dumpsters. Standing in the shadows were two McDonald's employees. Fadi froze in surprise. Through the gloom he could see that one of them was Noor. She leaned next to a tall, gangly boy with tattoos, drinking a soda while he showed her something in a magazine.

"See, told you I was right," he said with a wink.

"Man, I can't believe I lost our bet," grumbled Noor with a giggle.

The boy raised his hand, and Noor's palm smacked against his in a high five. The sharp sound rang through the back alley, and Fadi inched back. Noor grabbed the magazine and turned. Her eyes widened as she caught Fadi standing at the corner, and she started to cough.

"What's wrong?" asked the boy, pounding her back.

Fadi hitched up his backpack and ran. The honey tin thudded against his back, but he didn't stop till he opened the door to his apartment. He staggered inside and collapsed on the fraying couch. *Noor's going to think I'm spying on her. She's going to pound me for sure.*

That night Fadi and Noor avoided making eye contact as the family sat down for dinner.

"Here, Fadi, take the yogurt," said his mother, passing him the bowl.

"Thanks," murmured Fadi. Zafoona's eyes were dull, and deep shadows lay along her cheekbones. He knew she wasn't sleeping well ever since they'd heard from Professor Sahib, but at least she was coughing less. The doctors had diagnosed her with a serious chest infection, but the good news had been that it could be cleared up with a series of powerful medications. Unfortunately, the pills left her sleepy and groggy most of the time. Fadi took a spoonful of tangy homemade yogurt and plopped it onto his plate, next to a pile of stewed cauliflower. He hated cauliflower. But he knew they'd be eating a lot of it this week; it had been on sale at Save Mart, and his father had bought three heads.

"So, Fadi," asked Habib, "anything interesting happen at school today?"

Fadi shook his head. An image flickered in his brain, like a hazy still from a reel of film. It was Noor laughing intimately with the tattooed boy in the narrow alley behind the McDonald's.

"Come on," wheedled his father with a smile, "there must be something."

"Well," said Fadi, trying to erase the image and come up with something interesting to report. "There is a photo club starting next week," he mumbled in a rush.

"A photo club! That sounds wonderful," said Habib
with a twinkle in his eye.

That's a good one, he thought with relief.

"Boy, we used to have fun with that old camera in
Kabul," added Habib.

Fadi nodded. "The fee is fifty dollars to join."

Habib's smile faltered.

"Fifty dollars?" interrupted Zafoona with a frown.
"That's too much."

"Well, maybe—," said Habib, but Fadi interrupted
him.

"No, no, it's okay," said Fadi in a rush, wishing he'd
never brought the subject up. "I'm really not that interested. It's just that . . . well, there's just a club for photography, that's all."

Zafoona's mouth tightened and she glanced at Noor.
"Why did you waste money getting another pair of
earrings?"

Fadi glanced at his sister's earlobes. She was wearing
shiny new hoop earrings.

"They weren't very expensive," said Noor, her voice
low. She brushed her hair forward, hiding her ears. Her
fingernails were painted black.

"*Jaan,*" said Habib, "Noor works very hard. What's a
little jewelry for our pretty daughter?"

Zafoona's lips quivered and she remained silent.

Fadi looked around the table at his family, and guilt spread like acid through his gut. They all blamed themselves for Mariam's loss. They would hate him if they learned the truth.

Later that night, as the rest of the family retreated to their rooms, Fadi sat in the darkened living room staring at the square of light glowing from the tiny television. His father had bought it at a garage sale, and the remote control was missing, so he had to lean over to change the channel. None of the shows looked interesting, and he was about to switch it off when a story on the ten o'clock news caught his eye. A little girl traveling to New York from Chicago had gotten on the wrong flight and had ended up in Miami. As Fadi watched her happy reunion back with her parents in Chicago, he wished Mariam were on a plane coming home right then.

10
Stowaway

"YOU DIDN'T SHOW UP at photo club yesterday,"
a familiar voice whispered next to Fadi.

Startled, Fadi looked up to see Anh standing next to
his chair. "Uh, no," he said, minimizing the window
on the computer monitor. "I couldn't go." He sat in the
library, surfing the Internet, trying to find more news
stories about the girl who'd accidentally gotten on the
wrong plane.

"Well, you should have," she said, her almond-shaped
eyes earnest. "Ms. Bethune asked me about you—said
she'd seen you at the park with a camera and that you
really liked photography."

"Well, yes," said Fadi, rifling his brain for a good excuse. "But I have too much homework to do . . . and I have to help my father after school," he added lamely.

"That's too bad," said Anh.

"Well, thanks for telling me," said Fadi, trying to turn back to the computer.

"If you change your mind, you can still join. The real meetings don't start until next week anyway. Ms. Bethune has a lot of cool stuff planned for this year," said Anh. "There's a contest we're entering, cosponsored by the Exploratorium museum in San Francisco and the Société Géographique. It's open to students in the San Francisco Bay Area."

Fadi sighed. *I'd love to, but I don't have the money.*

"The first-place winner gets one of those new digital cameras and the opportunity to go on a photo shoot with a Société Géographique team."

"Wow," said Fadi, intrigued despite himself. *What an amazing opportunity.*

"Yup. You have the choice of going to the Great Wall in China, the Taj Mahal in India or on a safari in Kenya. You and a companion get to travel for free with room and board provided for a week."

Fadi froze. *A trip to India? India is right next door to Pakistan! I could fly into India and just hop over to Peshawar.*

Hope flared through him. "Really?" he tried to sound casual, but his voice squeaked. "A trip to India?"

"Personally, I'd do the safari, but yeah, you can choose. But you need to come to the next meeting and join the club," pushed Anh.

Fadi nodded. "I'll try."

"Okay, then. See you in art class," said Anh. "I'm checking these out for ideas." She showed him two glossy books. One was titled *Oceans of the World*, and the other had brightly colored fish on the cover.

"Great idea," said Fadi, happy to change the topic. *Too bad,* he thought. He knew if he entered the contest he had a good chance of winning. *But there's no way I can get fifty dollars by next week. Or ever.*

He turned back to the computer and typed in the URL for Virgin Atlantic. The plan he'd cooked up earlier that morning was going to have to come into play.

Fadi lay in the cramped, dark space trying not to make a sound. It smelled of old feet and moldy onions, so he breathed through his mouth. *Try to think of the wide-open skies. And fresh air,* he thought. He adjusted his legs so that his backpack lay snug between his knees. *This is it.*

This is my chance to go and find Mariam, and I'm not going to screw it up.

Once again Fadi was in a car, and like Claudia he was running away, again. But unlike Claudia, who had taken weeks to carefully plan out every aspect of her escape, Fadi was flying by the seat of his pants, coupled with a whole lot of praying. If he succeeded, he would bring Mariam back and reclaim his honor.

Fadi waited with his ear pressed against the floor of the trunk, trying to pick up sounds from outside. Right before he'd snuck out of the apartment, he'd spotted his father performing his evening prayers. After Habib finished, Fadi knew his father would grab his wallet, the car keys, and a warm coat like he usually did. Then he'd head out for a twelve-hour night shift at San Francisco airport. Fadi's mind wandered for a moment, mentally going over the items in his backpack.

The day before, Fadi had waited till his father and Noor were out of the house and at work. Then he'd gone down the hall to his parents' room and gently pushed open the door. He'd inched around the door frame and seen his mother taking her afternoon nap, hidden under a pile of blankets. Getting down on his hands and knees, he'd inched across the matted carpet and found the small black bag his father kept in the closet.

Holding his breath, he'd gone through folders of important documents and taken his passport and the airline tickets, saved from their trip from Peshawar. He planned to hold the tickets in his hand so that no one would question whether he was a real passenger or not. He was just hoping no one would actually look at the fact that they were used. He'd added a change of clothes, his toothbrush, and twenty-five dollars borrowed from Zalmay, all his cousin had had in the coffee jar hidden under his bed. He'd gotten Zalmay to swear he wouldn't tell anyone where he was until the adults figured out he was missing. The honey tin lay at the bottom of the backpack, a permanent fixture. *By then it'll be too late to stop me,* he thought.

As Fadi nervously ran his fingers along the inside edge of the trunk roof, he heard footsteps approach the car. Fadi held his breath as the echoing sounds stopped a few feet away from his head. A key jangled as it entered the lock. The driver's door opened with a quiet swoosh, then slammed shut. Fadi could feel the vibration of the engine as it rumbled to life. The radio blared, filling the back of the car with the sound of soft jazz. Within minutes the car pulled out of the apartment complex and headed toward the airport for a long night of shuttling passengers around.

Good! thought Fadi with relief. *Things are going according to plan.* Earlier that evening he had stuffed pillows into his bedroll and molded it to look like a human body. He wanted his parents to think he'd gone to sleep early. He'd turned off all the lights in the living room and hidden behind the couch. When the coast had been clear, he'd snuck out of the apartment and hidden in the trunk of the taxi, which he'd unlocked earlier.

Now all he had to do was wait for his father to drive to the airport and line his car behind the rest of the taxis waiting to pick up passengers. Then he'd use the safety toggle switch in the trunk to pop the lid. Yesterday, when his father had been taking his afternoon nap, Fadi had double-checked the trunk from the inside, making sure the safety release worked properly.

The tricky part was to make his way through the airport, pretending to be a passenger. He'd checked the Virgin Atlantic flight schedule and knew a plane was leaving for London at midnight. More than enough time to find a family and tag along, like an innocent kid flying alone for the first time. He'd gotten the idea watching the news story about the girl who'd gotten on the wrong plane. If she could get on the wrong flight, he was sure he could get on one going in the direction he needed. Once inside the airport all he had to do was make his way to the departure gate and sneak on board the plane. His plan wasn't fully fleshed out on what he'd do when he got to London, but he was sure he'd find a flight going to Peshawar from there. Now all he had to do was wait. So he made himself comfortable and tried to roll with the bumps as his father drove over the San Mateo bridge and up Highway 101.

Sweat ran down Fadi's back as he gazed down at Noor's glow-in-the-dark Mickey Mouse watch. He was sure she wouldn't mind that he'd borrowed it—when he called them from Peshawar with news that he'd found Mariam. It was 9:47 p.m. The car had been traveling for more than half an hour, so they would be reaching the airport any minute. He felt the elevation change and the car slow down, indicating that his father had exited the freeway. Fadi's body rattled around the trunk as Habib drove over a series of speed bumps. The brakes squeaked a little and the car came to a halt.

Fadi stretched his cramped muscles and tensed. It was almost time to make his move. He pulled the straps of his backpack over his arms and slid it on. He waited five minutes to see if the car doors opened. But it looked like his father wasn't getting out. *Good.* He flipped on the flashlight and groped along the side of the car, looking for the toggle switch that released the trunk. The light illuminated the gray interior, revealing a flap of fabric near the left taillight. The toggle switch was concealed beneath.

Fadi held the flashlight steady with his teeth and moved the flap with his left hand. Breathing heavily, he gripped the switch with his thumb and forefinger. With a quick prayer he pulled. His eyes glanced up at the lid of the trunk, waiting for it to pop open so that he could scramble out. But he didn't hear the familiar click of the mechanism releasing. It remained dark and the door stayed shut. *I'm doing it wrong.* Fadi got on his hands and knees and pulled the switch again. Nothing. He tugged it from side to side, then up and down. Nothing. *Calm down, you dork,* he berated himself. He took shallow panicked breaths. *What did I do differently yesterday?* He was trying to replay how he'd opened the trunk the day before, when the taxi bolted forward, tossing him against the back metal edge of the trunk.

"Ouch," he yelped. *What the . . . ?* Fear raced through him as he scrambled after the flashlight, which had rolled to the inner edge of the trunk. The car slowed again as Fadi aimed the light back at the switch. The car stopped. Perspiration collected along Fadi's forehead as he yanked on the switch. His fingers fumbled with desperation as he heard the driver's door swing open. Muffled voices discussed the weather, and footsteps approached the back of the car.

Oh, no! Fadi curled up in a ball and pressed his back against the inner edge of the trunk just as light spilled inside and two faces peered down at him.

11
Failure

FADI COULD SEE HIS FATHER'S EYEBROWS arch in shock as he stared down at him. The passenger he'd just picked up, an elderly Chinese man, looked down in surprise as well.

"Get out," said Habib under his breath.

Fadi quavered as the confusion on his father's face turned to anger. Fadi crawled out, grabbing his backpack, which had fallen off.

"I'm so sorry, sir," said Habib, turning to his passenger. "This is my son. If you don't mind, he will be riding in the front with me."

"No problem," said the man. "Very unexpected, but

what can we do with youth today?" He shook his head sadly. "All troublemakers."

The tips of his ears burning with shame, Fadi slunk into the front seat. He looked in the side mirror and watched his father place two heavy suitcases into the trunk. Meanwhile the crotchety old passenger let himself into the backseat and put his walking stick across his legs. Then he leaned back and closed his eyes with a deep sigh of exhaustion.

How am I going to explain this? Fadi cast a wary glance at his father. His stomach felt like it was on a wild roller coaster ride. Habib climbed into the driver's seat and pulled on his seat belt. He ignored Fadi, turned on his blinker, and merged with traffic exiting the airport. *Boy, am I in big trouble. What am I going to say?* Fadi turned his face toward the side window and stared at the airport disappearing behind them. A line of planes stood at the gates and on the tarmac, one of them painted with the bright red Virgin Atlantic symbol. *I'm such a loser. I couldn't even get out of the trunk, let alone get on a plane. I've failed Mariam. Again.*

The rest of the ride passed in silence as Habib drove north toward downtown San Francisco. Soon the soft sound of snoring filtered in from the back. The passenger had nodded off. For a moment Fadi's fear and embarrassment melted away as the taxi was shrouded in wisps of fog rolling in from the bay. Habib eased his foot from the gas, driving at a safer speed as light from the headlights bounced against the mist, creating a glow around the car. The fog ebbed away as they climbed a sloping hill. Coming around the peak, the city revealed itself with a burst of radiant light.

Fadi blinked in awe, taking in the sprawling landscape. Tall buildings strung with jewel-toned neon signs pierced the inky sky. Curving streets spread out in a grid, glittering with green, yellow, and red traffic signals. To the right Fadi could see the Bay Bridge stretching out toward Oakland, disappearing into plumes of fog. Pacific Bell Park sprawled below as they took an overpass, the park's bright green diamond empty. Habib drove through the financial district and headed up Divisadero Street toward the marina. It was a Friday night, and the sidewalks were full of people going in and out of restaurants and cafés. Habib exited the main thoroughfare and took a right into a quiet residential neighborhood. He stopped at a small house painted bright yellow.

"Sir, is this it?" asked Habib, a hint of worry in his voice.

"Yes, yes, it is," said the passenger, snorting as he blinked his eyes.

"Wonderful," said Habib. He pushed open the door to help the man with his luggage.

"Study hard, young man," said the passenger, bending down to look through the driver's window. He tapped on the steering wheel with his cane. "If you don't study and work hard, you'll end up a taxi driver like your father."

Fadi angrily opened his mouth but saw the look of warning in his father's face through the windshield. *How dare he? Doesn't he know my father has a PhD?* He wanted to grab the walking stick and snap it in two. Then the anger deflated. *Of course he doesn't know that my father has multiple graduate degrees. How could he? To the man, my father is just a poor taxi driver. And I'm his troublemaking son.*

Habib took his fee and got back into the car. Fadi looked at him under his eyelashes and was surprised to see a deflated expression on his father's face. Fadi's breath caught in his throat, and a sense of sadness wafted over him. He looked away as Habib pulled away from the house. Fadi braced himself for a tongue-lashing, but as the minutes passed, his father remained silent. Fadi cast a look at his father's tired profile and kept his mouth shut. Habib took a right back onto Divisadero and headed deeper into the city. He drove past a large hospital and pulled into a diner with a line of police cars parked out front.

"Uh, you're not having me arrested, are you?" said Fadi, sitting up straighter.

"Did you do something illegal?" asked Habib.

"No."

"Well, you won't be arrested, then," said Habib. He pulled his taxi into an empty spot in the parking lot. "Come on. I need some coffee."

Fadi followed his father into the busy restaurant, where a hostess in a beehive hairdo greeted them. A line of police officers sat at the counter, eating fried egg sandwiches and exchanging notes.

"Table for two, please," said Habib.

"Certainly," said the woman. Her eyeshadow was bright blue and sparkled.

"I have to call the apartment first to let them know you're okay," said Habib. He pointed to the phone booth. "You go ahead and sit."

Fadi nodded and followed the hostess to a small booth.

"Here you go, kid. Look it over," said the hostess. She handed him two menus. "I'll send over your waiter."

Fadi was halfway done reading the dinner specials when Habib returned.

"Are you hungry?" asked Habib.

Fadi shook his head. He looked down at his fingers

gripping the menu. There were traces of engine oil under his nails.

Habib flipped over his menu when a man in tight purple pants and an apron came by.

"What can I do you for, gentlemen?" he asked, holding up a pad of paper.

"Coffee for me, please," said Habib. "And a slice of apple pie and a glass for milk for my son."

"Good choice." The waiter winked. "It just came out of the oven, so I'll bring it over as soon as it's cut."

As the waiter hurried away, Habib turned his attention to Fadi. "Now tell me what you were doing in the trunk of my taxi."

Fadi gulped. He looked into his father's eyes. To his surprise, he didn't see anger. There was sadness there, mingled with concern.

Fadi wiped away a stray tear and opened his mouth. A torrent of words spilled out, explaining the whole harebrained scheme.

Habib took a deep swallow of coffee as Fadi finished his story. Then Habib paused for a few seconds, as if weighing his words. "So you thought you could go back to Peshawar and find Mariam?"

Hearing his father say it aloud made Fadi realize how stupid the idea had been. Reluctantly he nodded.

"Fadi *jaan*, I commend you for your desire to find Mariam," said Habib softly.

Fadi's head jerked up. *He's not yelling at me.*

"But what you were doing was illegal. You could have gotten into a lot of trouble. Even if you had gotten on the plane, you would've been caught when exchanging flights in London. If you had, by some miracle, gotten onto a flight to Peshawar, you would most assuredly have been arrested by immigration officers. Do you know you need a visa to enter the United Kingdom and Pakistan?"

"A visa?" said Fadi.

"A visa is a permit given by a country allowing a traveler to enter. It's kind of like getting permission to come visit. So, to go to London you would need a transit visa to travel through that country. Then you'd need a visa from the Pakistani embassy to go to their country."

Jeez, thought Fadi. *I didn't know that.*

"The probability of you succeeding with your plan was pretty much zero," said Habib. He didn't yell or get mad. He just stated the facts.

"Oh," said Fadi, feeling like a dumb donkey. Waves of embarrassment radiated through him. Even his ears were hot with shame. As the waiter came by and refilled

Habib's cup, Fadi glanced at the table next to them. A group of police officers chatted jovially, drinking coffee. Their black uniforms contrasted with the white and chrome tables, reminding him of the black-turbaned Taliban.

"But . . . ," whispered Fadi. "What if she's not found?"

Habib added four cubes of sugar to his coffee and stirred slowly. "She will be found," he said, his voice confident.

"How can you be so sure?" asked Fadi, expressing his worst fear, which he'd never spoken out loud.

"She will be found," repeated Habib, his lips compressed into a tight line. He paused a moment and looked Fadi in the eye. "I'm going to tell you something I haven't told anyone else."

Fadi gulped down his mouthful of pie and sat back in surprise.

"Can you keep a secret?" asked Habib.

Fadi nodded in a rush.

Habib twirled the spoon in his fingers, as if weighing his words. "After we found out that Mariam was picked up by that family, I sent Professor Sahib five hundred dollars."

"Five hundred dollars?" echoed Fadi. *Where did he get that kind of money?*

"I collected it from driving the taxi . . . and borrowed some," said Habib, as if hearing Fadi's unspoken question. "Professor Sahib and I have hired private investigators."

"Private investigators?" mumbled Fadi, imagining men in trench coats with magnifying glasses, skulking around for clues.

"There are men . . . ," murmured Habib, "ex–army officers, mercenaries, and drug runners, who can be hired to find out things. Hopefully they'll find information on what happened to Mariam after the truck left."

"Oh," said Fadi, hope flaring in his chest.

"It's no guarantee," said Habib, his voice grim. "Just have patience," he added, "and keep praying, for Allah answers our prayers, in one way or another."

Fadi nodded. *Patience and prayer. Not a very satisfactory answer.*

"Now, in regards to hiding in the trunk of my car," said Habib, his voice hardening. "That was one of the stupidest things you could have done. You could have been seriously hurt."

As his father lectured him on his foolish behavior, Fadi tried to put on a sufficiently sorry expression. He didn't mind the lecture one bit; his father loved him.

12
Catastrophe

NOOR WAS UP MAKING A CUP OF COFFEE for herself when Fadi and his father returned to their apartment the next morning. Fadi was exhausted but happy, and since it was Saturday, he could sleep in. He'd spent the entire night traveling around the city with his father. When the taxi had had no passengers, Fadi had helped his father memorize the stack of maps kept in the car's glove compartment. They'd both watched the sun come up over the Golden Gate Bridge, which Fadi was a bit disappointed to learn was painted red and not gold. After dropping off the last passenger in Berkeley, near the University of California campus, they'd returned home.

"Good morning, Noor," said Habib.

"Good morning, Father," said Noor. "Would you like some coffee?"

"No, thanks. I'm off to bed. By the way, I hope you didn't mention what happened last night to your mother."

Noor shook her head. "She's been asleep the whole time."

"Good." Relief flooded Habib's face. "No need for her to worry unnecessarily. . . . She has a lot on her mind as it is. I'll see you both later this afternoon, then."

Noor sipped her coffee and ate a slice of toast as Fadi handed his father his passport and the old tickets. Habib patted him softly on the back and went to the bathroom to take a shower before heading off to bed.

"Your bedroll is in my room," said Noor. She gave Fadi a calculating look that made him a little nervous. "Why don't you take a nap in there, and when my shift ends at one, come meet me. And bring my library books with you."

Fadi looked at Noor and wondered why she wanted to see him. But he was too tired to worry about it now. "Okay," he mumbled. "I'll see you then."

As he dragged his backpack behind him toward Noor's bedroom, he heard his sister's voice one last time.

"And put my watch back where you found it."

He put the Mickey Mouse watch on her nightstand and collapsed onto her bed. Within moments he was asleep.

Why did I ever agree to meet her? thought Fadi with growing trepidation. He pulled on the rumpled clothes he'd been wearing the day before and ambled into the kitchen for a glass of orange juice. *She's going to yell at me, then pound me. I just know it.*

But he had to face his sister sometime, and obviously the time had come. In a strange way he was looking forward to it—relieved that things were going to clear up between them, however things turned out. He put Noor's library books in a bag and left the apartment, after checking in on his mother. She was asleep under a pile of blankets, as usual; she was having trouble getting out of bed these days. *Khala* Nilufer had whispered to him the other day that although his mother's body was getting better, her mind was taking a lot longer. Plus, all the strong medications didn't help. They made her sleepy and out of sorts.

It was an unexpectedly cool day for the beginning of the second week of September, and Fadi shivered a little, wishing he'd thought to bring a sweatshirt. He jogged through the parking lot of a grocery store and headed toward Paseo Padre Parkway. He slowed as the McDonald's came into view. He came around the back, half expecting to see Noor waiting for him in the alley, but she wasn't there. *She's probably inside because of the cold.* He walked to the front door and held it open for an older couple to walk through.

He spotted Noor sitting at a table facing the front window, overlooking the main street. She looked pre-occupied, watching a group of kids go by.

"How was Mom when you left?" she asked as he pulled up a seat.

"Fine. Taking a nap," responded Fadi, grabbing the box of chicken nuggets she held out. She'd chosen his favorite dipping sauce—honey mustard.

"It's a good thing she doesn't know about your escapade last night," said Noor, giving him a measured look.

Fadi mumbled, his mouth full.

"Did you try to run away?" she asked point-blank.

Fadi started to cough, and Noor had to whack him on the back. "Not so hard," he complained. "And, no," he mumbled, "I didn't try to run away."

"What were you doing, then?"

Fadi chewed for a full ten seconds, took a sip of soda, and

finally answered. "I was going to go look for Mariam," he mumbled.

"Are you crazy? How were you going to do that?"

And for the second time in twenty-four hours Fadi explained his half-baked plan.

"Wow. That takes guts," she said, playing with her straw.

Fadi blinked. *She's not telling me I'm an idiot.*

"Idiotic for sure, but ballsy," she said, and grinned.

Fadi smiled back, bits of nugget between his teeth.

"Gross!" she yelled, throwing a french fry at him.

Fadi laughed and slurped some soda.

"So did Dad let you have it?" she asked.

"No, he was really nice about it. But he yelled at me for hiding in the trunk of his taxi."

"Well, yeah," said Noor. "You could have really hurt yourself."

"He has a lot on his mind," said Fadi softly. Both of them looked at each other, and then looked away. Mariam was there, hanging over them like a ghost.

"How come you haven't told them?" asked Noor in a quiet voice, interrupting his thoughts.

"Huh?"

"About Tom . . ."

"Who's Tom?"

"The guy . . . with the tattoos."

Then it dawned on Fadi what she was talking about. "Oh . . . him, the one you were . . . you were hanging out with in the back."

"Yeah," said Noor, turning pink. "He's not my boy-friend or anything like that," she added. "He's a senior at my high school, and he's going to the University of California, Berkeley, next year to study astrophysics."

"Wow, Berkeley." Fadi whistled. He remembered driving past the sprawling campus the night before.

"Yup, he's really smart. And very helpful . . . with different stuff."

"Well, it's none of my business."

"Thanks," she said. "It's just that I haven't made that many friends . . . and Tom is a really nice guy. Someone I can talk to . . ."

"My lips are sealed."

She looked relieved. "So," said Noor, changing the subject, "what's this photo club thing? A bunch of nerds clicking away?"

Fadi frowned. "No . . . it's nothing."

"It's not nothing, Fadi," said Noor. "I can see that it's important to you."

"It's a club where you learn how to take better pic-tures," said Fadi, his face stiff. "There's a competition.

The winner gets to go on a photo shoot. You can go to China, Africa, or India."

"India?" said Noor. Comprehension dawned on her face.

"Yup, India," said Fadi. "Right next door to Pakistan."

"Wow," she said with a whistle. "That's quite an opportunity."

Fadi nodded. "But its fifty dollars to join. . . . It's too expensive, like Mom said. We don't have that kind of money to waste."

Noor sat back, a calculated look on her face again. "I've seen the pictures you and Dad used to take," she said. "They were pretty good."

"Thanks, I guess."

"So you think you can win?"

"I'd try my hardest."

Noor pulled out her wallet and took out two crisp twenties and a wrinkled ten-dollar bill. "I'll give you the money."

Fadi eyed the money with longing. "I don't know," he whispered. That money could pay bills, help with the groceries.

"Take it," said Noor. She put the money into his hand with a conspiratorial smile. "I'm not trying to buy you off, you know."

Fadi grinned, the weight lifting from his shoulders. Hope flared in his heart again. *This is an omen. I know I'm going to win. I just know it.*

Fadi practically ran to school on Tuesday morning, Noor's money safely tucked away in an envelope in his backpack. He flew up the steps and jerked open the front door. He fairly skipped down the crowded halls on his way to homeroom. As usual, students were milling around the halls, whispering to one another. But the looks on their faces were different. Fadi glanced at the table the school tree huggers association had set up to raise money for a campaign to clean up local beaches. Their collection boxes, decorated with peace signs, stood unattended. They weren't laughing or joking around. They where whispering, and they look scared.

"Did you see the news this morning?" said a boy in a Giants cap.

Fadi slowed, pretending to adjust his backpack.

"Yeah, I can't believe it—," said the girl next to him.

"My mom freaked out," interrupted her friend. "She has family in New York and was trying to call them all morning."

They gave each other anxious looks as Fadi paused.

What is going on? he thought, a prickle of unease creeping down his spine. He hurried on to homeroom and took his seat. He had unfinished math homework to take care of.

Homeroom passed as usual, with Mr. Torres coming in late, wearing an orange-and-white striped sweater. "Good morning, guys," he said.

The room was unusually quiet as students took their seats. Mr. Torres stood at the board, looking a bit dazed. Moreso than usual. He opened his mouth to say something, then closed it. He shook his head while running his hand through his rumpled hair and reached for the day's announcements. Fadi exchanged a questioning look with Patty, who was passing notes to her girlfriends. He shrugged at everyone's weird behavior. All he could think of was going to photo club at the end of the day.

As Fadi exited language arts later that afternoon, he passed by the water fountains and spotted Felix shoving a small sixth-grader out of line to take a drink. Fadi hurried on, toward the cafeteria for lunch.

"You gonna buy me lunch today, rich boy," he heard Felix call out after him.

Pretending he hadn't heard, Fadi avoided the cafeteria, planning to hide out in the library. He passed the teachers' lounge and slowed down. The door was slightly open, and he could see Mr. Torres's loud sweater.

"I can't believe it," said Mr. Torres. "This was no accident. Two planes hit the Twin Towers and another crashed into the Pentagon."

"Oh, my God," came a woman's worried voice.

Fadi stopped, waiting to hear more. The door to the lounge opened and Principal Hornstein hurried out, smoothing the wisps of gray hair around his head. He gave Fadi a smile that didn't quite reach his eyes, and hurried toward his office.

By the time Fadi headed toward the art studio after school, he'd pieced together what had happened through fragmented conversations he'd heard throughout the day. Terrorists had crashed planes into two skyscrapers in New York and at the Pentagon in Washington, D.C.

Around a dozen kids were sitting in the art studio when he entered. Anh was there and smiled when she saw Fadi.

"Hey," she said. "You made it."

"Yeah," said Fadi. "I made it."

"So sorry I'm late," said Ms. Bethune. "I received some news. My brother works at the Pentagon, you see . . ."

She stopped for a moment, a blank look on her face.

"I heard kids talking about the planes," blurted an Indian boy. Then he snapped his mouth shut. His face looked a little green.

"Yes, Ravi," said Ms. Bethune, straightening her spine. "I'm afraid there's been an attack. . . . Planes crashed into the Pentagon this morning, and well, my brother called to tell us he was okay."

"Oh." Ravi gulped as the other students looked at one another.

"I'm sure you will discuss it with your parents when you get home," said Ms. Bethune. "I'm going to cancel photo club today, but I'll take your membership dues."

Fadi unzipped his backpack to remove his money. His hand brushed the honey tin, and he paused. The familiar square shape filled his palm, and he gently squeezed it before letting go. He pulled out the envelope and handed it to Ms. Bethune, who was passing around sheets of paper. Fadi's heart raced as he read the title: "Take Your Best Shot Contest Guidelines."

"Take these and read them at home," instructed Ms. Bethune. "If you want to enter the contest, you need to give me your pictures by October eleventh. I need to send them to Société Géographique by the twelfth. Next week we can discuss what you might want to photograph, and I'll give you guys rolls of film. The following Tuesday we'll start learning how to use the darkroom."

"Cool," murmured Ravi.

Fadi skimmed over the page and saw that the results of the competition would be announced December first, and the awards ceremony would take place in San Francisco the following week or so. He looked at the grand prize. The digital camera held no meaning for him. He wanted those two tickets to India. To do that he had to come up with something so original and awesome that it stood out from the rest of the entries. The rules said you could take pictures of anything; you could be as creative as you wanted to. *But what would win the competition?*

Culprit

BY THE END OF THE DAY, Fadi knew that the world as he knew it would never be the same again. He, along with Noor and his parents, sat around their tiny television, glued to the screen. Stark, horrific images flickered in the darkened room, bursts of orange, gold, black, and smoky gray.

"This is terrible, just terrible," whispered Zafoona. She sat on the faded brown recliner, wrapped in her shawl. Her eyes were rooted to the two majestic buildings on the screen. As flames exploded outward, the massive steel and glass structures faltered and Zafoona closed her eyes and turned away.

Noor leaned forward to flip the channel, but everywhere she clicked there was repeated footage of a plane, flying low, crashing into the second tower of the World Trade Center. "How can such solid buildings collapse?" she whispered. Gingerly her fingers touched the screen, as if trying to feel whether it was real.

"Leave it on this channel, Noor j*aan*," said Habib.

The host of CNN had assembled a panel of terrorism experts to share their theories on who could have carried out such a well-planned attack. It was nearly ten o'clock, time for Habib to head out for the airport, but he couldn't seem to leave his seat.

Zafoona's eyes snapped open. "This is a horrific deed. . . . So many innocent people are dead."

"Who did it?" Fadi wondered out loud. He leaned back against the recliner and folded his arms against his chest.

Zafoona reached down and brushed his overlong bangs away from his eyes. Her eyes cleared. "Whoever did this has no value for human life, and whatever statement they're trying to make is lost by their evil actions."

"Yes," said Habib. "This is an act against Allah and all of humanity. And there will be retribution."

Fadi heard the darkness in his father's words, and it

worried him. He reached for his mother's hand and felt
her fingers tighten around his.

The next day Fadi stood with his father in a grocery
shop in Little Kabul, watching long, flat sheets of freshly
baked bread, nearly as tall as he was, emerge from the
oven. They were fifth in line, waiting their turn to pick
up bread for dinner. Fadi's nose tingled as he inhaled the
pleasant smell of yeast and spices while glancing at Habib.
His father's face was troubled. Habib had called Professor
Sahib that morning and found out that the men they'd
hired hadn't found a speck of information on Mariam
or the family she'd disappeared with. *Five hundred dollars
down the drain,* thought Fadi glumly.

Shrugging off the feeling of disappointment, Fadi
turned around to inspect the back of the store. Usually
the store hummed with noise as people chatted, laughed,
and exchanged jokes with the tiny white-haired owner
who sat at his usual spot, next to the register. Today everything was eerily quiet. Fadi scanned the dry fruits aisle and
spotted Masood, one of the two Afghan boys from his
math class. Masood stood next to a table piled with cakes
and cookies. As if feeling Fadi's eyes on him, he looked up,
and his eyes met Fadi's. He nodded in acknowledgment.

Fadi returned the gesture. *Maybe I should go talk to him.* But he couldn't, since Habib had stepped away to pick up some canned beans, and he had to save their spot in line. Reluctantly Fadi turned his attention to a group of men huddled near the butcher's counter, dour expressions on their faces.

"Did you hear the news?" muttered one. An old scar ran down the right side of his face, giving his cheek an odd, puckered look, like he'd swallowed a lemon.

"No. What happened?" another man asked.

Fadi saw his father's attention turn toward the men as he returned to join him in line. Intrigued, Fadi's ears perked up.

"They're reporting that the nineteen terrorists were affiliated with Osama bin Laden and al-Qaeda," said the scarred man.

Fadi saw the woman at the head of the line turn pale. She took her bread, grabbed her little boy, and hurried over to the cashier.

"This is going to spell disaster for Afghanistan," said a third man.

Fadi stiffened. *This is not good. Osama bin Laden is in Afghanistan.*

"Once Osama was a hero." A man in a leather jacket sighed. "He helped defeat the Soviets."

"I know!" interrupted the scarred man. "We all have wounds from that war. But now Osama has turned against the United States."

"Well, the Taliban have offered Osama *panah*, so he's not leaving Afghanistan anytime soon," said the butcher.

He's right, thought Fadi. According to the Pukhtunwali code of *panah*, or asylum, if a person asks for protection against his enemies, the person, in this case Osama, would be safeguarded at all costs.

"This spells big trouble," said the butcher. He handed the scarred man a packet of meat. "It is not good that outside elements, like al-Qaeda, are ruining Afghanistan."

"They are working with those villains the Taliban," grumbled an older man with a cane. "We need to get rid of them both."

Fadi saw his father frown. Others in the store stopped what they were doing and looked toward the butcher.

A tall man with narrowed blue eyes paused as he was exiting the door. His large hands gripped the bags in his hands and he turned toward the men. "The Taliban you are cursing are the ones who brought order to the country," he said.

"They are religious zealots," responded the older man. "They have made Afghanistan the laughingstock of the world. Now they are working with Osama."

The blue-eyed man took a step forward, his fists clenched. "Once the Soviets left, the country was overrun by warlords. Do you want to return to that? Seventy percent of Kabul was destroyed, and hundreds of thousands of Afghans were killed. That includes every ethnic group—the blood of Pukhtuns, Tajiks, Hazaras, and Uzbeks filled the streets. The Northern Alliance is made up of the same warlords and will bring disaster to Afghanistan."

The man with the cane stiffened. "Well, the Taliban are doing the same now."

The blue-eyed man took another step forward, his lips pursed in a tight line.

"Brothers, stop!" shouted a voice next to Fadi.

Fadi jumped, blinking in surprise. It was his father.

"We cannot go on fighting among ourselves!" said Habib. His strong, deep voice rumbled through the store.

Fadi cringed, wanting to dive behind the ten-pound rice bags. All eyes in the store were on them.

"No one is perfect. We have all made mistakes— Pukhtuns, Tajiks, and others," continued Habib. "We need to come together as Afghans now, for the sake of our country." He turned to the blue-eyed man. "You are right, Brother. The Taliban brought order to the country when it was needed." Then he turned to the group of men. "Before the Taliban came, the Tajiks, Uzbeks, and others were destroying the country. But now the Taliban are doing the same. They are working with Osama bin Laden, who is using Afghanistan for his own agenda."

"He's right," muttered an old woman. Her hair covered by a white scarf, she stood next to the nut bins.

The men next to the butcher harrumphed and walked away, while the blue-eyed man swung his bags around and left the store.

"There will be trouble in Afghanistan," prophesied the old woman. Then, as if nothing had happened, she went back to inspecting pistachios, sold by the pound.

A sense of foreboding drifted over Fadi. *Things are going to get worse. I just know it.*

14
Target

"LOOK! IT'S OSAMA," shouted a familiar rough
voice.

Fadi stepped out of the boys' bathroom and froze like
a rabbit hearing a hawk. The door squeaked shut behind
him. He gazed down the hall, looking for the source of
the voice. But the hall was bare, with only a few stragglers rushing to class before the bell rang.

"Why aren't you with your towel-headed friends?"
growled the voice again.

Fadi inched away from the bathroom. He looked
past the water fountain and noticed that the door to
the janitor's closet was ajar. Before he could run, two

figures emerged from the dark interior.

Felix stepped out to stand next to Ike. "Yeah, we don't want you camel jockeys around here."

Fadi's stomach clenched as he surveyed the nearly empty hall. The last student gave him a pitying look and slipped into his classroom.

"What?" said Ike, twisting his lips. "Cat got your tongue?"

"No. A camel got his tongue," Felix said, and sniggered. He balled his right hand into a fist and hit it against his left palm. An expensive gold watch hung loosely on his wrist.

"I don't want trouble," squeaked Fadi, edging backward. He stopped. If he went back into the bathroom, he'd be trapped.

"'I don't want trouble,'" mimicked Ike in a high-pitched voice. "You asked for trouble when your terrorists attacked us."

"Let's show him some American-style justice," muttered Felix.

Fadi gulped. He eyed the hall to the right, toward his math class. It was too far away. The closest door led to a seventh-grade classroom. He could make it if he darted quickly past the boys and ran fast. He was about to bolt forward when Principal Hornstein stepped out from around the corner. His old checkered tie hung loose around his neck, as if he'd been pulling at it.

He looked quizzically from Fadi to Ike and Felix. "Any problem here, boys?"

"No. We just needed to take a leak," said Ike, as if everything were normal.

"And you?" asked Principal Hornstein, turning toward Fadi.

Fadi's throat was dry, his tongue stuck to the roof of his mouth. He looked at Ike and Felix, who were standing like innocent choirboys. "No," he finally mumbled. "No problem."

"Good," said Principal Hornstein. "You two go to the bathroom, but make it snappy."

As Ike and Felix swaggered into the bathroom, Principal Hornstein turned to Fadi with a contemplative look in his eye. "Is everything all right, son?"

Fadi nodded a little too fast. *Keep it cool.* "Yeah, everything is fine," he said.

"Well, if you have any trouble, or need to talk to someone, you know where my office is."

Fadi nodded and scurried to math class.

A few minutes later Ike and Felix wandered in behind him.

"You're late!" said Mrs. Palmer in exasperation. Her

curly red hair swirled in a halo around her head as she scribbled on the blackboard.

"Principal Hornstein said we could go to the bathroom," said Ike with an insolent smile.

Mrs. Palmer paused for a moment and sighed. "Okay. Sit down."

Ike gave Fadi a pointed look and slumped into his seat.

Fadi opened his backpack and pulled out his notebook just as Mrs. Palmer put down her chalk and turned back to the class.

"Okay, class. Close your textbooks. It's time for a pop quiz!" she announced.

The students groaned. Along with the others Fadi took out a sheet of paper with shaking fingers. Hunched over the desk, he settled down to sort out improper fractions. He could feel Ike's and Felix's eyes boring into his back. He was going to have to be super careful to avoid them. The consequences were too painful to think about.

Fadi and Anh were in the studio, waiting for Ms. Bethune to show up for art class. Anh leaned across the table toward Fadi and pulled a stack of printouts from her binder. "I did some research," she said.

"What kind of research?" asked Fadi. His mind was still on his run-in with Ike and Felix earlier in the day. He felt like a mouse being hunted by sharp-clawed cats. It wasn't a good feeling.

"Research about the competition," said Anh.

"Oh," said Fadi, picking up the scent of her watermelon-flavored lip balm. *Nice,* he thought, then blinked in embarrassment.

"Are you all right?" asked Anh.

"Yeah, I'm fine," said Fadi. He looked at her and wondered for a moment if he should tell her about Ike and Felix. *But she can't help really, so why bother?*

"Okay. Well, my dad always tells me to be one step ahead of the game," she said, looking pleased with herself. "Yesterday I went online and dug up information on the Take Your Best Shot competition . . ." She trailed off with a smile.

"And . . . ," said Fadi, waving his hand.

"And I found the names of the four judges."

"Isn't that kind of like cheating or something?"

"Nope," she said, tossing back her hair. "It's public information since it's listed on the competition's website, under rules and regulations."

"Oh," said Fadi, impressed.

"Once I got the names, I dug up more information about them."

Fadi leaned over the table, shielding the sheets from the group of kids that had wandered in. One of them was Ravi, from photo club.

"Here's the first judge, Millicent Chao," she whispered. She flipped through the printouts. "She's the director of the Exploratorium."

Fadi looked down at the smiling face of a middle-aged woman in a pink pantsuit. Her lengthy bio was attached. As Fadi skimmed the paragraphs, he learned that Millicent Chao was a graduate of Stanford University and had double majored in architecture and East Asian history. She was married and had a daughter who was a dancer with the San Francisco Ballet. She enjoyed taking apart clocks and putting them back together again, cooking experiments, and horticulture, especially growing bonsai trees.

The second page was the home page of San Francisco City Councilman Henry Watson. He was fluent in Spanish and Portuguese and owned a Brazilian restaurant in the Castro. He liked to read, surf, and travel, especially to South America. Next was Lauren Reed. She was the regional manager for Kodak film, and there wasn't much information about her, or even a picture.

The last judge was Clive Murray, a photojournalist from the Société Géographique. He was a world-renowned "image maker" and had won countless awards. Anh had stapled a bunch of sheets about him together, including a bunch of his pictures. Fadi read that Clive's trademark photography style was "capturing the essence of human diversity, cultures, struggles, and joy." He had worked in every corner of the earth. He had covered a lot of conflicts—including the Iran-Iraq war and the crises in Cambodia, Rwanda, and the Congo—and he had followed the plight of refugees in Sudan, Iran, India, and Pakistan.

Wow, Fadi thought, looking at some of the photographs Clive Murray had taken. Some of the most arresting images focused on people—portraits of children at play, women cooking, and old men sitting in contemplation.

He looked at Anh in awe. "This is really awesome, all of this research." He handed the stack back to her, but she pushed it back.

"This is your copy," she said. "Now all we have to do is figure out what they like and make sure our pictures appeal to them."

"Thanks," said Fadi. "You're really amazing." He slipped the pages into his backpack, his mind churning with hundreds of possibilities of what to shoot.

"Look, I've heard you talking to Ms. Bethune about angles, light, speed, and all that other photography stuff. It really sounds like you know what you're doing," she said. "I'm pretty good at doing research and investigating. So how about you help me with my photography and I'll keep you loaded with information?"

"That's fair," said Fadi. He grinned. "You help us figure out what to shoot, and I'll help us shoot it."

"Great," said Anh. "That sounds like an awesome plan."

Fadi gave Anh a grateful look from under his eyelashes. This was really going to give them a leg up on the others. *Man, she's really like Claudia,* he thought. While at the Metropolitan Museum of Art, Claudia and her brother had tried to solve the mystery of one of the statues, given to the museum by Mrs. Basil E. Frankweiler. The first thing Claudia had done was go to the library on Fifty-third Street and do research on the famous Renaissance artist Michelangelo.

"Where's Jon?" wondered Fadi. He looked around for their missing partner.

"Oh, he's out with some viral thing," said Anh. She pulled out the library books she'd shown him in the library.

"Oh," said Fadi. "That's too bad." Jon tended to be sick a lot, poor kid.

"No, he's not," said a girl on Anh's left. She was from homeroom, Patty's friend, whose name he could never remember.

"What?" asked Anh.

"Rumor has it Jon was jumped by Ike on the way home from school," said the girl. Her eyes were bright at sharing a juicy tidbit of gossip.

Fadi gulped. "Are you sure?"

"Yup," said the girl with a nod. "Ravi saw it happen. Ike took Jon's collection of DVDs."

"Oh, man," said Anh. "Was he hurt badly?"

"No, just shook up. But you know Jon."

"Yup," said Anh. They did. Jon tended to get hurt easily.

Poor guy, thought Fadi.

"Sorry I'm late," said Ms. Bethune. She walked through the door and put down her bag. "We need to get cracking on our collages today since I want to finish this project before Thanksgiving."

Fadi flipped open the book on undersea life and examined the bold colors of the tropical fish. He blinked, forgetting Jon for a moment as he noticed how the photographer had captured a bright orange and black clown fish nestled in a pale sea anemone. The fish practically popped off the page.

Fadi remembered what his father had taught him while they'd roamed the hills of Kabul, exploring birds' nests and finding colored rocks. The three key ingredients of a photo were simplicity, composition, and lighting.

The photographer who'd taken the picture of the clown fish had captured all three elements in one picture; he'd chosen the image of a single fish and not cluttered up the picture with too much other *stuff.* Since you couldn't use a telephoto lens underwater, he'd probably zoomed in and cropped the shot tighter. His composition of the shot was impressive. He'd used an artist's technique called "the golden mean" to divide the picture into imaginary thirds both vertically and horizontally, like a tic-tac-toe board. Then he'd placed the subject of the photo, the fish, on or near those imaginary lines or their intersections so that the orange and black fish popped against the pale tentacles of the anemone.

Fadi knew that great photos almost always showed a skilled use of light. The best photos were taken at dawn, in the late afternoon, or at dusk, when the low angle of the sun produced rich, warm colors and long shadows.

You needed to avoid shooting at noon, a time when light was "flat." It could seem very complicated, but for Fadi, once a camera was in his hand and he was looking through the viewfinder, it all fell into place. Then, with one click you could capture an amazing image.

Now I just need to figure out what that amazing image is. Fadi sighed. One amazing image that would get him to Peshawar.

15
Barbie

HABIB MANAGED TO FIND an empty parking spot at the back of the lot and squeezed his taxi in between a delivery truck and a Mercedes-Benz. "Come on, *bachay*," he said, turning back to Fadi and Zalmay, who sat in the backseat. "We don't want to be late for Friday prayers."

Zalmay nodded happily. It was his birthday, and Habib had promised to take the boys to Toys"R"Us after prayers to pick out a present. Fadi followed Zalmay and his father through the parking lot toward the blue and gold tiled facade of the mosque. Stragglers took off their shoes and said their *Salaam*s to friends and hurried inside. Fadi paused at the front step to unlace his tennis shoes. After taking them off, he slipped them into the shoe rack and walked inside. The mosque had just opened, and he could smell the faint scent of fresh paint in the wide, airy prayer hall.

"My dad donated money to build this mosque," whispered Zalmay, puffing out his chest.

Fadi looked around, impressed. No expense had been spared by the Afghan community to construct the majestic building. The main hall could accommodate more than five hundred, and its rising minarets announced prayers five times a day.

"There," whispered Habib, pointing to the right.

Uncle Amin had managed to save them a spot before things had gotten too crowded. The trio made their way across the soft carpet and sat down.

The imam shuffled toward the front of the building and the *mihrab*, which pointed toward Mecca. His long, fluffy white beard hung down his chest, and a prayer cap covered his bald head. He settled his rotund frame onto a prayer rug in front of the crowd and cleared his throat into the microphone. It was a hint to quiet down before his *khutba*, or sermon, began.

"I hope he doesn't talk about smelly socks again," whispered Zalmay, elbowing Fadi.

Fadi muffled a giggle. Last week the imam had talked

for more than an hour about Allah's love for cleanliness and purity of both body and soul. His jowls shaking with emotion, the imam had spent ten minutes telling people not to come to the mosque wearing smelly socks or after eating garlic because that disturbed the prayers of people around them.

He had a point, thought Fadi, eyeing the clean white socks of the man in front of him. His nose wrinkled. *I don't want to kneel next to smelly feet.*

"I thought long and hard about what I should speak about today," began the imam. His usually animated voice was subdued. "My mind kept coming back to the events of Tuesday, for it was a terrible, terrible day. It was a day of killing—a day of violence."

An uncomfortable silence filled the air. The audience sat still, many with their eyes downcast, as if in meditation.

Boy, we're not talking about smelly socks, thought Fadi. *I kind of wish we were.*

"But as I thought about who the perpetrators were, or why they had done these deeds, I kept coming back to a *surah* in the Holy *Qur'an.* The verse, number thirty-two, is in chapter five. And before we talk about anything else, I feel we need to think long and hard about what this verse means."

The imam cleared his throat, and soon the hall was filled with melodious Arabic, the language of the *Qur'an*. The imam paused a moment, then translated. "We ordained for the Children of Israel that if anyone slew a person—unless it be for murder or for spreading mischief in the land—it would be as if he slew the whole people: and if anyone saved a life, it would be as if he saved the life of the whole people."

He followed the translation with ten seconds of silence, allowing the words to fill the cavernous room.

"So, brothers and sisters, what the *Qur'an* is saying is that if we kill one human being, it is as if we have killed all of mankind, and if we save a human, it is as if we have saved all of mankind. That is the point we must understand. When you kill, you cease to be a true human."

Fadi stood in a daze as the sliding doors closed behind him. His mind was still back at the mosque and on the imam's sermon. It had reminded him of the importance of human life, and of its value. A shiver of unease settled over him as he stared out into the sprawling store. Dozens of beady eyes stared back at him from the line of stuffed circus animals on sale.

"Fadi, come on," prodded Zalmay. His cousin pushed

him past the greeting cards and wrapping paper.

Fadi looked away from the stuffed animals with a shake of his head. He'd never seen so many toys in his entire life. Aisles filled with all kinds of gadgets, puzzles, and games stretched in every direction. He stood at the end of an aisle, paralyzed, not knowing which direction to turn.

"You get something as well, Fadi *jaan*," said Habib. "Something small, though," he added with a wink.

"This way," said Zalmay. He dragged Fadi past the toy trains.

Fadi wanted to stop, to check out the intricately laid-out tracks, the towns, bridges, and water tower, but Zalmay had a set destination in mind.

"Uncle Habib, we'll be in the electronics section," Zalmay called out.

Habib smiled and waved them on.

They jogged through aisles of puzzles, past the bicycles and the sports equipment. Kids ran through the store, tossing balls at one another, laughing happily. A little girl drifted behind her mother, her arms overflowing with princess dresses, glass slippers, and a sparkling tiara.

Fadi stumbled for a moment, eyeing the girl's bright pink dress. *Mariam's favorite color.*

"Here," said Zalmay. He pulled Fadi into the video games section.

Fadi blinked anxiously and turned away from the girl to watch his cousin's eyes widen at the row of new releases.

"Wow," Zalmay said breathlessly. "The new Super Mario! And Space Invaders Five! You're going to love that one. I played it at a friend's house last week."

Zalmay walked up and down the aisles, checking out different games, reading the descriptions and the reviews.

After a few minutes Fadi got bored. "I'm going to check some stuff out," he called out to Zalmay. "I'll be back."

Zalmay waved at him distractedly while talking with the sales assistant about the superiority of Myst over Civilization.

Fadi wandered through the stuffed animal shelves, amazed at how lifelike they were. He patted an electronic dog that waved its tail and barked. He passed by the superhero action figures, remembering a lot of them from Saturday morning cartoons. He paused at the X-Men figurines and looked them over. Neat, but no, he didn't want to spend money on one. Hoping to find his way back to the board games, he turned the corner and stopped dead in his tracks.

From both sides of the aisle hundreds of Barbies stared down at him. Fadi closed his eyes. His body felt cold and his hands went numb. He swallowed, feeling thirsty all of a sudden. His eyelids flickered open. Cowgirl Barbie gave him an accusing glare. Artist Barbie stood next to her, holding a paintbrush, sharing a conspiratorial frown with Doctor Barbie. Fadi's chest tightened and he glanced downward. Assembled on the bottom row stood a platoon of Barbies from around the world. Native American, Korean, Spanish, Nigerian, and Austrian Barbie were whispering to one another . . . whispering about Gulmina.

The memories he'd kept hidden away in the back of his mind came like a flood, threatening to drown him. Fadi stumbled forward. He needed to get out of the aisle. He dragged his leaden feet, begging them to cooperate, but the row of Barbies seemed to lengthen, stretch out for miles. He gulped, his throat parched. *Pink. There are so many kinds of pink* . . . Beach Barbie carried a coral-hued towel, Movie Star Barbie drove a fuchsia jeep, Ballerina Barbie twirled in a pale pink tutu. Unbidden, an image flared in front of him. It was Mariam, holding out Gulmina, asking him to put her into his backpack. *And I didn't do it.* He could practically feel Mariam's tiny fingers slipping away from his as the phantom rumble of a truck echoed in his mind.

Hot anger flared from his mind and rippled through his body with a surge of heat. He glared at a smiling Barbie in a fluffy lavender dress, and his hands balled into fists. *It's her fault*. He heard a scream echo through the store, not realizing that it came from his own throat. Anger overcame reason and he launched himself into the display case. He knocked off a line of dolls, and they crashed to the floor. He stomped on the slender rectangular boxes, his tennis shoes making crunching sounds. He fell to his knees and ripped off the lids and pulled out Diamond Princess Barbie. He shook her with all his might and started banging her and Soccer Barbie against the concrete floor.

The store manager found him, huddled on a pile of crushed boxes and Barbies, sobbing. It was the woman with the little girl in hot pink who had spotted him tearing apart the Barbie section. After Habib was located, the two men disappeared into the manager's office. When they returned, Fadi saw the understanding and compassion in the store manager's face. Fadi hadn't caused a lot of damage, but they had to buy four of the Barbies, whose arms and legs had snapped off. Zalmay gave the dolls an odd look when he saw their purchase, but he was too excited about his own gift to ask why Fadi had chosen a bunch of Barbies.

Fadi sat at the edge of the *dastarkhan*, across from Zalmay and his other cousins. He'd pulled his hair forward so that no one could see the purple bruise on his forehead from where he'd hit his head against the metal frame of the Barbie display case.

Everyone was unusually quiet as *Khala* Nilufer and his mother passed out plates of food. Fadi glanced at the empty spot next to the sliding doors that led to the backyard. It was where Uncle Amin usually sat. But he wasn't home yet. A huge chocolate cake with twelve candles sat on the coffee table, waiting for later. But he wasn't in the mood. Only Abay and Dada seemed oblivious to the undercurrent of tension. They sat together, having an animated conversation about some jewelry Dada had bought for her when they had first gotten married. In their rush to leave Kabul, she'd left it behind. Now she was joking with Dada that he should get her a new necklace. She pressed her lips and pretended to be angry. Fadi couldn't help but smile at Dada's hopeless shrug. Sometimes they acted like newly-weds, and it was kind of embarrassing to watch.

Noor arrived from work and sat down next to him. "What's up?" she asked.

Fadi looked into her curious eyes, and his heart constricted. *I want to tell her. I need to tell someone about Mariam and Gulmina.* "I beat up a bunch of Barbies at Toys"R"Us," he whispered.

"You did what?" she asked. Her brows shot up.

Fadi's heart raced. "Look . . . I know it was stupid, but—" Before he could confess, Uncle Amin walked through the door, his face grim.

Khala Nilufer dropped the basket bread on the *dastarkhan* and spun around. "Amin *jaan*," she said, "is it true?"

Uncle Amin ran a hand over his sparse hair and glanced at the kids. "Yes, but I'll talk about it later."

An awkward silence filled the room as the kids gave one another questioning looks.

Sahar, one of the younger cousins, leaned forward and puffed out her chubby cheeks. "Someone beat up poor Mr. Singh," she said in a garbled whisper.

"What?" said Zalmay.

"Mr. Singh, the ice cream truck man," said Sahar, her eyes round. "I heard Mama telling *Khala* Nilufer."

"Someone beat up Mr. Singh?" Zalmay burst out.

Uncle Amin exchanged a pained look with the adults.

"Why would someone do that?" asked Zalmay.

"He's such a nice man," said Fadi, all thoughts of a confession evaporating.

"Oh, my goodness," grumbled Uncle Amin, looking at his wife.

"They're going to hear about it from other people," said *Khala* Nilufer with a deep sigh. "Tell them what happened. It's important they hear it from us."

Uncle Amin sat down next to the sliding doors and grabbed a glass of water. He took a long drink before speaking. "Last night Mr. Singh went to the warehouse to pick up a shipment of ice cream, like he usually does," he said. "He was getting back into his truck when he was attacked by two men."

Fadi stared at him, his eyes wide. He had a feeling he knew what was coming.

"He was attacked because the men thought he was a Muslim since he wore a turban and beard. They blamed him for what happened on September eleventh."

"But he's not a Muslim," said Zalmay, near tears. He'd known Mr. Singh for many years and had received many gifts of free ice cream.

"I know, Son," said Uncle Amin. "But the attackers didn't know, or care, I suspect. They were mad over what had happened and they wanted to take it out on someone they assumed was a Muslim."

"How is he?" asked Fadi. He remembered seeing Mr. Singh that last time, handing out ice cream to kids near Lake Elizabeth. He felt numb.

"He's in the hospital with broken ribs and a concussion," said Uncle Amin. "That's where I was, visiting him and his family. The doctors say he'll recover in a few weeks."

"Mr. Singh's family must hate us," said Noor, her voice soft.

"No, of course not, Noor," said Uncle Amin.

"But he was attacked because they thought he was one of us, a Muslim," pressed Noor.

"No, no," interrupted *Khala* Nilufer. "Mr. Singh's family would never blame us for what happened to him."

"Children," said Habib. The seriousness in his tone quieted everyone. "The attacks in New York and Washington have frightened people very badly. They are scared and angry, two emotions that can sometimes make people do terrible things. I want you all to be careful. If you have any problems at school with people bothering you or calling you names, tell your teachers, or come to us."

"Your uncle Habib is right," said *Khala* Nilufer. "If anyone says anything threatening to you, tell us at once."

Fadi nodded along with the rest of the kids.

"Come on, kids. Time for lunch," said Zafoona with a cheery smile that didn't quite reach her eyes. "We've got a delicious cake for later."

Fadi looked at the worry in Uncle Amin's face. It was the same worry Fadi had been carrying with him since Ike and Felix had caught him in the hallway and called him a towel head. He looked at Noor's worried expression and dropped the subject of beating up Barbie. He wasn't so sure he wanted to tell her about it now anyway.

16

Exposure

"THE DARKROOM IS NOT A PLACE to hang out and chitchat!" came Ms. Bethune's exasperated voice from outside.

Fadi exchanged a grin with Anh as she locked the darkroom door behind them. A lot of pictures had been ruined that afternoon when eager club members had opened the door, exposing undeveloped prints to light. But the two of them weren't taking any chances. Anh had noticed that you got more time when all the other students were done, so she'd reserved the last slot on the darkroom schedule. Plus, you had Ms. Bethune all to yourself if you had any problems.

"You go first," said Anh. She pulled out her negatives and peered down through a magnifying glass. "I can't decide which pictures to develop."

Fadi nodded. A week, a mere seven days, a paltry one hundred sixty-eight hours remained till their deadline. Ten thousand, eighty minutes to turn in the perfect shot to Ms. Bethune. The pressure was on. He said a quick prayer and gently unfurled the negatives from the roll of film he'd shot over the weekend. His shoulders tense, he slipped the reel inside the enlarger's cartridge. The enlarger was brand new and far easier to operate than the one his father had had back on Shogund Street. But the process was the same, and he quickly figured out how to work the lens so that it projected the negative's image down onto the easel. He scrolled to the third frame. A contented sigh whistled through his lips as he squinted down to examine the image. *There it is.*

He'd gotten the idea for the picture from his last trip with his father to San Francisco, when he'd been busted trying to stow away on a plane to Peshawar. Images of the city with its rolling hills, curving streets, and colorful neighborhoods had lingered in his mind, reminding him of how he and his father used to walk the hills of Kabul, taking pictures of the city below.

With a sense of nervousness Fadi had approached his

father one afternoon when they'd been alone in the apartment together. He'd told Habib that Noor had given him the money to join the photo club.

"Really?" Habib had said, looking at Fadi over his reading glasses.

"Uh, yes," Fadi had said.

"That was very nice of her," Habib had replied as he returned to memorizing the street map of Oakland.

Relieved, Fadi had told his father his idea for the winning shot. His eyes twinkling with interest, Habib had agreed that it was a marvelous concept. He let Fadi come with him to work the following weekend, and when he'd finished his shift at six a.m., they'd strolled through the city, eating chocolate doughnuts, joking, and—best of all—taking pictures.

Fadi now adjusted the knobs on the enlarger, bringing the image into focus. The blurry gray lines sharpened, revealing a shot of Fillmore Street. He'd taken the picture in the crisp morning light, looking down from a steep hill as the street shot down at a nearly ninety-degree angle, stopping at the sparkling waters of the San Francisco Bay. The lighting was perfect. The neat thing about the slope of the street was the restaurant signs that jutted out from the graceful buildings on each side. There was a Chinese restaurant, a German *hofbrau*, a

Mexican *taqueria*, a falafel joint, a sushi bar, and a French bakery.

The composition of the shot works, thought Fadi. *I hope the judges like it.*

The director of the Exploratorium, Millicent Chao, studied architecture, which the picture showcased. The buildings in the photo were restaurants, and Councilman Henry Watson owned one. Both of the judges loved the city, and the picture highlighted San Francisco. He wasn't sure what Lauren Reed liked, since they had never been able to get much information about her. And Clive Murray? Well, Fadi was sure he'd like it too, since the different restaurants represented ethnic and cultural diversity. He cropped the picture, cutting out the buildings along the edges so that the eye would follow the street down to the water. The eye naturally read the restaurant signs, creating the feeling of travel, passing through the world of food.

Fadi turned off the enlarger and grabbed a sheet of eight-by-ten photo paper. He slipped it under the lens and turned the enlarger back on. Light flashed down through the negative, landing on the paper. Within a minute, the machine automatically turned off.

Fadi exhaled, not realizing he'd been holding his

breath. He removed his negatives and put them away. Next he retrieved the photo paper and turned to Anh.

"All yours," he said.

As she fiddled with the enlarger, Fadi carried the photo paper over to the "wet" area of the darkroom. Ms. Bethune had prepared chemical baths in three trays and set them up in the long metal sink. He used tongs to place the paper in the first tray, containing washing chemicals. This was a delicate process, and the sheet could only remain in the solution a minute; too long a soak resulted in the paper breaking down. Fadi set the timer and stared down through the red gloom.

When the timer rang, Fadi reset it for five seconds and used the tongs to pull out the paper and slip it into the indicator stop bath. The print next went into the fixer for two minutes, which would make it light safe. Fadi gently pulled out the print and shook it to get rid of the solution. He attached it with film clips and hung it up to dry. Now all he had to do was wait, so he went over to help Anh with her prints.

Fadi glanced from his picture of Fillmore Street back up to Ms. Bethune's contemplative face. "What do you think?" he asked. He and Anh had hurried to the studio at lunch the next day to check how their prints had turned out after drying.

Ms. Bethune pursed her lips and reviewed the glossy black-and-white image. Fadi gazed down at the photo, and self-doubt crept into his heart.

"You've really captured a stunning image, Fadi," said Ms. Bethune. "The idea of San Francisco being a cultural mosaic—literally a collage of different cuisines—is very clever. Technically it's beautiful, and it's executed perfectly."

"But it's missing something, isn't it?" said Fadi. His brows furrowed as his finger traced the street down to the glittering water of the bay.

"Don't be so hard on yourself," said Ms. Bethune. "It is a solid entry."

"No," said Fadi. He shook his head as it dawned on him what it was. "You've said it to us a hundred times. Great photos say something about life; they tell a story. My picture does that. But you've also told us that great photos evoke emotion."

"Well, yes, I have said that, haven't I?" said Ms. Bethune. She frowned, looking back at the photo.

Fadi glanced over at Anh's picture. Since the beginning she'd wanted to take an action shot. After reviewing the judges' backgrounds, she'd decided to take a picture of performers dancing the South American tango. Millicent Chao's daughter was a ballet dancer, and Henry Watson liked everything South American. She was sure Clive Murray would like the action shot, since many of his pictures focused on movement.

So Anh had dragged Fadi all over town to dozens of dance studios. She'd begged the instructors to let her photograph them. Finally, when a charming woman had invited them to a dance competition she was hosting, they'd jumped at the opportunity. Anh's father had dropped them off early to set up and had given them a big thumbs-up. An action shot required perfect timing and careful handling of the camera, so Fadi had suggested that Anh use a tripod. As Anh had nervously inspected the windows to establish the best source of light, he'd mounted her expensive, brand-new Nikon to the tripod and positioned it on the edge of the parquet floor. He'd admired the camera's sleek design and its cool new features.

As the dancing had begun, Anh had perched next to the performers. Her right eye had peered through the viewfinder while her index finger had hovered next to the shutter release button. With Fadi's help she'd kept the camera focused on a particular spot, at the center of the hardwood floor, waiting for the whirling dancers to enter the frame. Fadi had suggested using a fast shutter speed to freeze the action as it came into view. By the end of the competition Anh had shot three rolls of film.

The image she'd chosen showed a lean woman in motion, her shimmering dress whipped around her limber body as a man in a tuxedo dragged her across the dance floor. Light flowed in from the back window, illuminating the couple, highlighting the tension in their passionate embrace. Fadi peered down at the intense image captured on paper. It made him feel as if he were eavesdropping on the story of two lovers.

"This is an amazing picture," said Fadi with an appreciative sigh. "It captures all the key elements."

"Thanks," said Anh. Her eyes were troubled. "But, Fadi, you've got a great shot at winning too."

"No," said Fadi, his mind made up. "I don't think this is it." He took his print of Fillmore Street and tore it up.

"Are you sure?" asked Anh.

"Yeah, I'm sure," said Fadi.

"Well, it's up to you," said Ms. Bethune. "But you've got a week to find the perfect idea and one last session in the darkroom."

Fadi nodded. He had to win that trip, and that required the best picture possible. *Second best isn't going to cut it.*

"Fadi, wait," Anh said as they left the studio. She pulled on his elbow, slowing him down. "Why is winning so important to you?"

Fadi stopped and turned back to look into her concerned face.

"Look, I don't mean to pry," said Anh, "but it seems like winning this competition means more to you than just a camera and a trip on a photo shoot."

Fadi paused and finally mumbled, "I really need to win that trip."

"Why?"

Conflicting thoughts flooded Fadi's head. Anh was a good friend, and he couldn't lie to her. He pulled her into a quiet nook and told her about Mariam, but left out the part about how it was his fault she was lost. Without saying a word Anh reached over and gave him a hug. Fadi hugged her back awkwardly, his nose tickled by long strands of silky hair.

"It wasn't your fault, Fadi." She sniffed and wiped her eyes with the edge of her sleeve. "As my father says, it was fate. When he and my mom left Vietnam on a boat fleeing the war, they got separated. But they found each other again in a refugee camp in Cambodia and came to America together."

"Oh," said Fadi, pulling away from her embrace.

"One of us is going to win," she said with confidence. "And you're going to get that trip."

Fadi didn't know what to say, so he just smiled. His heart felt lighter than it had in a long, long time.

17
Broken

"SO HOW'S YOUR PICTURE TAKING coming along?" asked Noor. She slipped her pencil into her biology book and peered down at him from the dining room table.

"Not so good," said Fadi with a weak smile. He sat on the floor, inspecting the inside pocket of his back- pack. He'd already overturned the bag and scattered its innards all over the shaggy olive green carpet. The honey tin skidded to a halt next to the three-legged coffee table. Fadi quickly threw a notebook onto it so that Noor wouldn't ask what it was. The roll of film Ms. Bethune had given him that morning was nowhere in sight. *Darn*. He'd planned on using it over the weekend.

"Not so good doesn't sound too good," said Noor. "What happened?"

Fadi paused, hating to admit his last picture had been a failure. He sat back and sighed. "I thought I had come up with the perfect picture when I went to San Francisco with Dad. Now I'm not so sure."

"Is there anything I can do to help?"

"No. You've helped me enough already," said Fadi. He unzipped the side flap and poked around. "You gave me the money to join the club. Now it's my responsibility to win the contest." No film hidden among his pens and pencils. *I definitely left it at school. Double darn.*

"Fadi," said Noor, her voice an octave lower, "I know you're an excellent photographer. You know all the tricks Dad taught you, but don't be too disappointed if you don't win."

Startled, Fadi looked up at her and frowned. *What does she mean, if I don't win?*

Noor held up a hand. "Now, don't get me wrong. You probably have a better chance at winning than anyone else. But . . . "

"I'm going to win," said Fadi, his voice stiff.

"Okay, okay," said Noor. "I'm sure you will."

Fadi stuffed everything back into his bag. "I just need to come up with an amazing concept. Something unique . . . something that tells a story, is full of emotion, and connects with the viewer."

"How about me?" said Noor. She struck a model's pose and batted her eyelashes.

"I want to win, not lose," said Fadi. He gave her a mock grimace.

"Look here, you little twerp," said Noor, shaking a fist at him. "Well, if you win that trip to India, it would be awesome."

Fadi looked down the hall toward his parents' bedroom. His mother had barely come out all week. There'd been no news about Mariam for more than three weeks now.

Noor caught his wandering look and pursed her lips. "*Khala* Nilufer is coming later this afternoon. She's taking Mom shopping."

"That's good. She needs to get out," said Fadi. He shook off a feeling of unease.

"Tell me about it," said Noor. Her lips twisted in frustration. "Her health is fine now. She's not doing herself any good by lying in bed all day long."

"I know, especially when we have to eat Dad's cooking," added Fadi.

They looked at each other and grinned, though worry still lurked in their eyes.

Fadi zipped up his backpack. "Look, I left the film Ms. Bethune gave me at school. I'm going to go back and pick it up and then go to the lake for some inspiration."

"Okay, but don't be late. I'm cooking dinner."

Fadi pretended to gag and ran out the door as Noor threw a tattered cushion at him.

Fadi stood on his toes and felt along the top shelf of his locker. At the right corner he felt a familiar cylindrical shape. *There it is,* he thought with a sense of relief. He grabbed the roll of film and stuck it into his back pocket. *Now I've got six days to find that great shot. No pressure. Yeah, right.*

He closed his locker with a muffled clang and headed back toward the front door. The only sound in the empty school was the slap of his tennis shoes against the checkered floor and the drone of the janitor's vacuum coming from the teachers' lounge. Fadi stepped outside and looked up at the sky. *Still another three hours till sunset. Good. Perfect light to experiment.* He'd landed on the bottom step when a sharp rustle in the bushes along the side of the building caught his attention. He paused a second, then sped up. *Probably just a couple of cats. But let's not take any chances.* He jogged toward the back of the school, which was the fastest way to get to Lake Elizabeth. He'd just rounded the corner when two guys burst through the bushes in a flurry of leaves.

"Catch him!" sounded Ike's familiar growl.

Crud, thought Fadi. He leapt forward, toward the parking lot, and broke out into a run. His backpack thumped against his spine as he looked back. Ike sprinted after him, with Felix a few feet behind, brushing dried leaves from his hair. There were only two cars in the lot since school had ended hours before. His heart thumping wildly, Fadi reached the middle of the lot, passed an old station wagon, and swerved around a little red hatchback. He paused, breathing in short gasps. The lot was enclosed by a metal fence, and the gate that led to the side alley was closed. *Double crud!* Someone had locked it for the weekend.

"You head him off!" shouted Ike. He ran past the station wagon and pointed to Felix to go along the back.

"Oh, no," whispered Fadi. He inched toward the hood of the tiny car, looking for someone, anyone, to help. The alley behind the school was desolate, and so was the playground. *I've got to get back to the front of the school and make a run for it.* He circled past the headlights as Ike reached the back of the hatchback. As Ike came up the side, Fadi ran, flat out, back the way he'd come.

The distance back to the front of the building seemed miles away, and in his haste Fadi faltered, tripping on loose gravel. As he slowed, he caught sight of a side entrance, used by faculty and staff. Regaining his balance, he bolted sideways, coming to a stop at the double doors. He yanked on the handle. It was locked. He pounded against the sturdy metal. "Help!" he shouted, his voice a hoarse rasp.

Ike had circled around the hatchback and raced toward him. Fadi pushed off from the door and ran. But Ike was too fast for him. He grabbed Fadi's shirt from the side and yanked him back. Off balance, Fadi stumbled while Ike tackled him onto the rough asphalt. Fadi sprawled on the ground, scraping his hands and knees as he went down.

"Got you, you little terrorist," hissed Ike, his breath hot against Fadi's ear.

With his face plastered against tiny fragments of gravel, Fadi saw shiny red and white high-tops pounding toward him.

"Way to go, Ike!" crowed Felix. While Ike held him down, Felix ripped off Fadi's backpack.

"Let's see what we got in here," he said, and sniggered. "A bomb? A manual for flying airplanes?"

"Let go of me," said Fadi. He turned back toward the boys. Scratches ran along his left cheek. "Why are you doing this?" he yelled. "I haven't done anything to you."

"Shut up," growled Felix.

After unzipping the bag Ike violently shook it, dumping out its contents. The photography books went flying out first, followed by his pencil case and the honey tin.

"No!" Fadi yelped in horror as his Minolta XE tumbled out last. As if in slow motion, the camera sailed through the air and hit the black asphalt with a sickening crunch. Broken parts flew in all directions as a huge crack appeared in the lens.

Noooo! I need that to win the competition! Blind rage flowed through Fadi, fueling a sudden burst of energy. He spotted Mariam's tin box and he growled—a deep, guttural animal sound. He twisted around and grabbed Ike by the shoulders. With superhuman force he pulled him down. Before Felix could react, Fadi used his legs to flip Ike to the ground and scrambled on top of the redhead's stomach.

"How could you do that?" he shouted, tears of rage

slipping from his eyelashes. With balled fists he swung. He got in a good punch or two before Felix pulled him off. Fadi twisted in his grasp, bent sideways, and bit Felix on the shin.

"Ow!" hollered Felix. He dropped Fadi like a hot potato and grabbed his leg. Fadi lunged forward and drove his head into Felix's stomach, knocking the wind out of the boy. They both tumbled to the ground.

"Why, you little . . . ," yelled Ike.

As Fadi and Felix wrestled on the ground, Ike grabbed Fadi's legs. Fadi held on to Felix, and soon all three boys were a mess of arms and legs, rolling around the parking lot. As Fadi felt a punch to his jaw, he heard the rattle of doors open.

"Stop it right now!" ordered a high-pitched voice.

From a gap between Felix's leg and Ike's elbow Fadi caught a glimpse of the old white-haired janitor. The man dropped his trash bags and hurried toward them.

"Stop this instant, you ruffians!" he huffed.

"Let's go, man," panted Ike. He got in a last punch to Fadi's side and pushed away.

Fadi held on to Felix's leg as Felix tried to get up.

"Get off me, you camel turd," howled Felix.

The janitor had nearly reached them when Felix twisted away and ran after Ike, who'd climbed over the back fence. All Fadi could see were the broken pieces of his camera lying on the ground. *It's broken.* His heart sank.

"I'm going to have to report this to Principal Hornstein," said the janitor, eyeing Fadi with suspicion. "Fights on campus are serious business, young man."

Fadi nodded. He didn't care how much trouble he was in. He showed the janitor his ID, but claimed ignorance on the other two boys' identities. As the man returned to his trash bags, Fadi picked up his stuff, along with the pieces of his camera, and headed home.

October 7th

NOOR FOUND FADI HIDING in the darkened bathroom, behind the shower curtain. He sat in the tub, cradling his broken camera in his arms. She flipped on the lights and leaned over the side of the tub. Her eyes widened seeing his puffy face, but it was the blotches of blood spattered on the front of his T-shirt that made her scream. Within seconds their parents burst into the cramped orange tiled room.

"Oh, Allah, have mercy," cried Zafoona. She pushed past Noor and knelt next to the bathtub. Habib followed close behind.

Zafoona and Noor pulled Fadi up out of the tub and settled him on the toilet.

"What happened?" asked Habib.

Still in shock Fadi barely felt the pain as his mother grabbed his face and turned it toward the light. "A couple of guys jumped me as I was leaving the school," he said.

"If I get my hands on those boys . . . ," growled Zafoona, her eyes lit with fire. Then her face softened and she kissed Fadi on the tip of his nose.

Habib's lips tightened as he rifled through the medicine cabinet. He took out a dark bottle of peroxide and bandages and placed them on the counter.

Fadi looked up at Habib with teary eyes. He held out the camera, his hands shaking. "They broke it, Father. They broke it."

Habib took the camera and knelt down. "Don't worry about it, *jaan*. The most important thing is that you weren't seriously hurt."

Noor's eyes narrowed. "Did they try to rob you?"

Fadi blinked. "No," he mumbled.

"Did they call you names?" pushed Noor.

"Yes," said Fadi. "They said I was a terrorist."

Silence descended in the cramped room.

"Fighting is not the answer, Fadi *jaan*," his father said. "It never solves the problem."

Zafoona shook her head in anger and stood up. She took cotton balls out of the jar next to the sink and grabbed the bottle of peroxide.

"I know, Dad," said Fadi. A flare of anger went through him. Ike and Felix had attacked him, and he hadn't done anything to them to provoke it. He wanted them to suffer, like he was suffering.

"Who were they?" asked his mother. She dabbed at his face with a cotton ball soaked in peroxide.

Fadi winced at the stinging. "I don't know who they were," he said. *I can't tell them. Dad's going to drag me to school, and my name will be mud for ratting them out. Then I'll really get it.*

"Are you sure?" asked Noor. "Have you seen them around in the school?"

"It's an awfully big school," mumbled Fadi. "I've never seen them before."

As the three of them fussed over him, Fadi's thoughts shifted to the competition. How was he going to enter without a camera? There were only six days to submit the winning shot.

"Your face still looks awful," whispered Noor. She sat next to Fadi in the backseat of the car as Habib drove

down Thornton Avenue. "I should have put some con-
cealer on it."

"No way," grumbled Fadi. "You're not coming any-
where near me with makeup." He gingerly touched his
swollen lip and let out a pent-up breath. It was their
parents' wedding anniversary, and for once Habib didn't
have to drag Zafoona out of bed so that they could go
out for dinner. It was as if his getting beaten up were
the medicine his mother had needed to shake off the
blanket of sorrow that had been suffocating her. Fadi
was glad to see her coming out of her funk, but he was
in no mood to celebrate.

It had been two days since he'd returned home from
the fight at school. Forty-eight hours since his camera
had been smashed to pieces. Two thousand, eight hundred and eighty-eight minutes since the moment his
chance to win the competition had evaporated. One
hundred seventy-two thousand, eight hundred and
eighty-eight seconds since he'd failed Mariam, yet
again. *There's no denying it. I'm a complete loser with no
honor.* Anger burned through him, and he hungered for
badal. He didn't care what his father said; Ike and Felix
had taken something precious from him, and he wanted
revenge.

Habib pulled the taxi next to a restaurant called

Khyber Pass. It turned out that the restaurant's owner, Gul Khan, was one of Habib's classmates from Kabul University, where Khan had studied biochemistry. They'd run into each other at Friday prayers and become reacquainted. Gul Khan had come to California years before and opened the tiny family-run restaurant off Peralta Boulevard in Little Kabul.

As Fadi followed his family inside, they were greeted by a short smiling man with a curved mustache. He bound forward and gave Habib a crushing hug.

This must be Gul Khan, thought Fadi. He peered around the cozy space, covered with red and black carpets and paintings of the Afghan countryside. Traditional music played softly from the stereo in the back.

"*Salaam Alaikum*, Brother Habib, Sister Zafoona," cried Gul Khan. "Welcome to my humble restaurant. And these must be your beautiful children."

Fadi ducked his head and mumbled his *Salaam*s.

Gul Khan seated them at one of the six tables in the practically empty restaurant. The only other customers were an older American couple, reviewing the laminated menu through bifocals.

"Business has been slow." Gul Khan sighed. "You know."

They all nodded. They knew.

"At least my store is secure," added Gul Khan under his breath. "A few stores down from me there's a carpet shop owned by a Pakistani man. It was vandalized the other night—the windows broken . . . awful things written in spray paint."

"These are difficult times, Brother Gul." Zafoona sighed. "We must be strong and vigilant."

"You are right, Sister, you are right," responded Gul as he handed them menus.

Fadi was happy to see that there was a sparkle in his mother's eyes tonight. She had made the effort to do her hair and had put on some lipstick, with Noor's urging.

Gul Khan's wife was in the kitchen, which could be seen from the dining area through a long rectangular window. She stood over bubbling pots, stirring. When she saw them look in, she hurried out to greet them.

"My wife makes the best *mantu* in town." Gul Khan beamed as his wife blushed.

"Then we will definitely have it," said Habib.

As the family settled down, Gul Khan's teenage son brought a starter salad to their table, along with glasses of *dogh*, a yogurt drink filled with chopped cucumbers and mint.

"Smells wonderful." Habib sniffed in appreciation.

"Yes, it does," said Zafoona with a rare smile.

Gul Khan came by to collect their orders, and within minutes their table was overflowing with hot fragrant food. Fadi avoided the plate of *mantu* and chewed on a piece of tender grilled chicken, watching the American couple awkwardly dunk bread into their eggplant dip.

"How is everything?" asked Gul Khan as he came around to refill their water half an hour later.

"Delicious, Brother Gul," said Zafoona. Her cheeks were pink, and she'd eaten most of the food on her plate.

Gul smiled with pride and paused when the phone rang. "One moment, please," he said, and hurried over to pick it up. He stood quietly, listening to the caller at the other end. As the seconds passed, he grew agitated. "Oh, Allah, have mercy," he whispered. His eyes darted back toward the kitchen. He hung up the phone and reached over to the stereo. He switched off the tape and adjusted the knobs on the radio.

Soon an English-accented voice of a BBC reporter filtered through the room.

"Brother Habib," said Gul Khan in a hushed voice. He hurried over and stood at their table, twiddling his fingers. "Listen to what is happening."

Fadi put his fork down, and his ears perked up to the details spilling from the commentator's lips.

"Tomahawk cruise missiles were launched from both U.S. and British ships this evening, signaling the start of Operation Enduring Freedom. This was accompanied by a mix of strikes from land-based B-1 Lancer, B-2 Spirit, and B-52 Stratofortress bombers. The initial military objective, as articulated by President George W. Bush, is to destroy terrorist training camps and infrastructure within Afghanistan, the capture of al-Qaeda leaders, and the cessation of terrorist activities."

Fadi hunched over his plate as his appetite evaporated. He watched his parents' faces pale as they all imagined the falling bombs. *Were they bombing Jalalabad? What about Mariam?*

19
Refocus

FADI FELT LIKE A hairy single-celled paramecium, immobilized under a microscope, squashed between two plates of glass. He wished he could fly right out the window, but he couldn't. Trapped, he sat in a slippery vinyl chair under Principal Hornstein's probing gaze.

"So, boys, what are we going to do about this?" said Principal Hornstein. He leaned forward on his desk and intertwined lean fingers with tufts of brown hair growing at the bases.

Fadi held his tongue and glanced to his right. Ike slouched next to him, inspecting his fingernails. He, too, said nothing. Principal Hornstein had sent the school secretary to call both of them into his office fifteen minutes earlier. Ignoring a feeling of impending doom, Fadi had felt a surge of satisfaction as he'd seen Ike's face. The redhead's lip was still puffy from where Fadi had clobbered him. A flame of anger went through him. *He's just a bully. I'm not going to let him beat me.*

Principal Hornstein sighed. "The janitor told me there were three boys involved in the fight. Two ran away, and one stayed, which was Fadi. Now, Ike, the janitor recognized you. He'd seen you snooping around his supply closet, but he couldn't place the other boy. So, why don't you tell me who he is?"

Fadi waited, watching Ike fidget in his seat. *I could tell Principal Hornstein*, he thought. *I could get them both busted for attacking me . . . for breaking my camera . . . for ruining my chance to win the competition.*

Ike looked down at his feet and mumbled. "It's a guy I know from Cesar Chavez Elementary, across town."

"I see," said Principal Hornstein. He leaned back in his chair with raised eyebrows. "And what is his name?"

"Leo," said Ike, a bit too quickly. "I don't know his last name."

Principal Hornstein turned to Fadi. "Do you know this Leo?"

Fadi took a deep breath. Felix's name was on the tip of

his tongue, ready to tumble out. "No, I don't," he said.

Ike straightened in his chair, blinking slowly. Fadi caught Ike staring at him, Ike's pale gray eyes narrowed. Fadi gave him a cold stare in return. *I'm not a tattletale, and I'm not going to get even through Principal Hornstein.* Ike frowned and looked away.

"The janitor mentioned the boy was Asian?" prodded Principal Hornstein.

"I think Leo's, uh, Filipino—uh, Korean, or something," fumbled Ike.

"I see," said Principal Hornstein. "So No-Last-Name-Leo is Filipino or Korean or something. I'll have to call Principal Jackson over at Cesar Chavez and see who this Leo is."

The two boys sat still, not moving a muscle.

"Without any cooperation I'm left with no choice. The policy for fighting on school grounds is set—three days suspension, starting today. I'm going to have to call your parents, so why don't you both take seats outside."

Fadi bristled at the unfairness of it, but remained silent. He pushed off from his seat and stalked to the door, elbowing past Ike. As he'd sat simmering in his chair, his mind had been working overtime. He'd come up with a plan, and he needed to put it into action.

· · · · · · · · · · · · · · ·

As Fadi waited outside Principal Hornstein's office for his father to pick him up, he asked the secretary if he could use the bathroom. At her curt nod he headed toward the art studio. He had to talk to Ms. Bethune. He didn't care if he was busted if they caught him; he was on a mission. He had a little more than eighty hours left, and somehow he was going to enter the competition.

Ms. Bethune saw Fadi enter, and she froze. "Fadi!" she exclaimed. "Oh, my goodness! What happened?" She put down the painting she had been about to hang up, and hurried over.

Fadi gave her a brief version of what had happened, leaving out Felix's involvement.

"And they broke your camera?" asked Ms. Bethune.

"It's completely destroyed," said Fadi with a deep sigh. His eye glinted with anger, and the bruise on his temple throbbed.

"I'm so sorry, Fadi," whispered Ms. Bethune. She patted him on the shoulder. "Look, I think maybe you should tell Principal Hornstein that you didn't start the fight—"

"No," said Fadi. "I'm sorry, but . . . I can't do that."

"You've put me in a tough spot, Fadi," said Ms. Bethune. "I need to tell Principal Hornstein what I know."

"Can you just . . . pretend you don't know anything, please?" whispered Fadi.

Ms. Bethune let out a deep sigh. "Well, I guess I'm not lying to save you from getting caught or receiving punishment," she thought out loud. "If you want to be punished for something you didn't do, I guess I could keep quiet . . . though I don't like it."

"Thanks, Ms. Bethune," said Fadi with relief, and changed the subject. "I'm still going to enter the competition."

"Well, you can borrow the photo club practice camera," said Ms. Bethune. She unlocked her desk drawer and pulled it out.

"No, I won't need it," said Fadi. The club's camera didn't work properly since so many students had fiddled with it over the years. "I just wanted to request some more time, if possible."

"Well, I was going to collect the pictures on Thursday, after school. After putting the packet together, my goal was to mail it out Friday."

"Can I give you my photo on Friday? It's just that I need a day to take the picture, process the negatives, and then develop the print in the darkroom, the day I come back from suspension. Oh, and get it to dry."

"Well, considering the circumstances, I think that

would be okay. But I need your entry form and photograph no later than by end of day Friday."

"Thank you, Ms. Bethune," said Fadi with a heartfelt grin. Now he had to ask a good friend for a favor. That, and figure out what to shoot.

Later that night Fadi poked at his chicken stew with his bread as the family sat for dinner. He glanced at his father's exhausted face from under his eyelashes and felt a stab of guilt, coupled with shame. After his talk with Principal Hornstein, Habib had driven Fadi home. While stopped at the railroad crossing, he'd turned to Fadi and asked what had happened. So Fadi had told him the truth, even about Felix. Habib had shaken his head sadly, and asked if Fadi would reconsider telling Principal Hornstein the truth. When Fadi explained that he couldn't, Habib surprised him by accepting his decision.

He knows it's about honor, thought Fadi, feeling even worse. He watched his mother stir the yogurt, her face solemn, thoughts adrift. Fadi knew her mind was wrapped up in the recent bombing of eastern Afghanistan. It was breaking news all over the television. Habib hadn't wanted to burden her with news of

Fadi's suspension, so it was to be their little secret. He'd be spending the next two days at the Fremont library, keeping up with his schoolwork.

Fadi looked across the small dining table and smiled slightly as Noor gave him a wink. For a moment, despite all the chaos swirling around him, his heart felt full. He was thankful for his family, thankful that they were safe. The emotion caught him off guard. He saw his father squeeze his mother's hand, and she gave him a glimmer of a smile in return. As he chewed on a piece of bread, Fadi smiled. He knew exactly what he was going to shoot.

20
Portrait

DUSK APPROACHED with lightning speed, casting a muted purple hue over the backyard. As the shadows lengthened on the ground, Fadi hurried to get ready. A mere half-hour window remained to capture the image before him. He pressed the latch on the right side of the camera and opened its back. Fadi popped in a new roll of film and threaded it into the take-up spool. He paused a moment to run a finger along the camera's sleek, shiny lines—so different from his old beat-up Minolta. He cast a grateful look over at Anh as she helped him organize the photo shoot.

No time to waste. He snapped the back of the camera

shut and chose the appropriate shutter and aperture set-
tings, which controlled the amount of light the film
would be exposed to. Shooting at this time of day was
tricky, and he needed artificial light to balance out the
fading glow of the sun. With *Khala* Nilufer's permission, Fadi and Zalmay had dragged two tall lamps onto
the patio. Zalmay had plugged them in and positioned
them behind Fadi's back, on the right. The illumination
from the lamps accompanied the fading sunlight, while
the slight angle of the lamplight created soft shadows
across his subjects.

Fadi shot Anh a thankful smile as she pulled her
tripod out of the duffel bag. She'd arrived fifteen minutes earlier, dragging her camera and equipment with
her.

"Do you need another lens?" asked Anh.

"No, this one works great," said Fadi, grabbing the
tripod. To accommodate the muted light, Fadi needed
to hold the camera as steady as possible and use a longer
shutter speed.

"Are you ready?" Fadi called out to the two people
sitting in front of him.

"I think so, *bachay*," said Dada.

It had taken Fadi half an hour to convince Uncle
Amin's elderly parents, Dada and Abay, to pose for him,

but finally they'd agreed. It was flipping through Clive Murray's bio that had given Fadi the idea to do a portrait shot. He'd read that of all subjects, people made the best photographs, since nothing fascinated humans more than looking at other people. A good people photograph showed character and emotion, creating a bond with the viewer. And Abay and Dada had amazing character in their faces. Years of marriage, love, loss, trials, and tribulations were written in every wrinkle, line, spot, and curve of their faces. Their faces were maps of their lives.

Dada sat a bit stiffly, looking around at the equipment with a frown. He wore traditional Afghan clothes, and a bright, colorful cap covered his balding head. Abay sat next to him, shrouded in a gauzy white scarf, as if hiding from the camera. Fadi had positioned the couple on a low bench, framed in the back by the shadow of overgrown rosebushes. He knew that, unlike the human eye, photographic film didn't easily handle bright whites and stark blacks. So the shade provided by the bushes created various tones of gray that were easier for the film to absorb. Fadi added the flash to brighten his subjects' faces.

"Anything more I can do to help?" asked Anh.

Zalmay hovered behind, carrying extra film.

"No, it's perfect. Thanks," responded Fadi. He shooed

the younger kids back to the sliding glass doors. They'd tumbled out of the house, intrigued by all the commotion. With curious eyes they watched, sucking lollipops Fadi had given them to gain their cooperation.

Fadi looked through the viewfinder and framed Abay and Dada in the little square. But he didn't want to fall into a pitfall many photographers fell into—shooting a subject's entire body, head to toe. He knew that when taking a portrait shot, the face, especially the eyes and mouth, were the key elements. So Fadi fit Abay's and Dada's heads into the shot and pulled back. He stopped when he'd cropped them to their shoulders. The viewfinder sought each line in Abay's and Dada's faces, which told the tale of the life they had led, filled with joy, pain, challenge, and triumph. He pressed the shutter button and took a dozen or so shots.

Something isn't quite right, he thought. Abay and Dada were too formal. They appeared uncomfortable, like they didn't want to be there. "Abay, Dada," he called out. "Please try to relax. Think of something fun, something funny maybe."

Dada nodded and smiled while Abay lowered her scarf from around her mouth. She looked at the camera nervously. Fadi took a couple more shots. These were better. But not great.

"Sahar," he called out. "Can you do a dance or something for Abay and Dada?"

Sahar puffed out her cheeks and shook her head.

"Look, I'll get you guys ice cream from Mr. Singh's truck."

The kids looked at one another and whispered. Fadi tapped his foot, looking up at the darkening sky.

"Two ice creams," said Sahar.

Highway robbery, thought Fadi, but agreed. Time was running out.

The kids stood under the lamps and started acting like monkeys, howling and hooting, scratching under their arms.

Abay and Dada laughed at their antics and relaxed a bit.

Darn. Not the look I'm going for. But Fadi continued to shoot. In the middle he replaced the roll with a fresh one. Finally, as the sun was about to sink into the horizon, he called it a night. This was it. As good as it was going to get.

"Thank you, Abay, Dada. I'm done," Fadi called out.

Relieved, the elderly couple stood up from the bench. In the process, Abay's scarf got caught in the rosebushes. Dada grinned, revealing a strong set of white teeth. With gnarled hands stricken with arthritis he gently unhooked her scarf and broke off a large yellow bloom and handed it to her. Abay giggled like a young girl and took a sniff of the rose.

Fadi froze. *This is perfect.* He refocused the lens and started clicking just as the sun fired a last burst of golden light over the yard before fading into the horizon. Abay and Dada were oblivious to those around them as they chatted softly to each other. *Click. Click. Click.* Abay's face was wreathed in happiness as Dada smiled. Elation flooded Fadi's heart. He knew that these were some of the best pictures he'd ever taken.

Fadi carried his lunch tray through the rowdy cafeteria, oblivious to the noise around him. He'd just handed his entry form and picture to Ms. Bethune, five hours before his deadline. He was exhausted and thrilled at the same time. *I'm going to win. I just know it.*

He stopped near the vending machines and spotted the table he usually sat at with Anh, Jon, Ravi, and a couple of other kids from photo club. It was empty. He was the first one there. He was about to sit down when he heard his name being called from behind him. He turned, peering across the table with the basketball players, next to the science fair geeks.

"Fadi," repeated the voice.

A group of boys sat next to the band kids. The one who had called his name was Masood, the Afghan boy he'd seen at the market the day his father had had his outburst.

"Hey, Fadi," said the other Afghan boy from his math class. "Aren't you a Pukhtun?"

Fadi froze. He realized that they were both Tajiks. The entire table was Tajik or Uzbek. They probably wanted to beat him up after what his father had said. Sweat beaded between his shoulder blades. They probably blamed the problems in Afghanistan and the attack on the United States on the Taliban and the Pukhtuns. He gingerly put one foot back, ready to turn around and run.

"Fadi," repeated Masood. He impatiently waved him toward the table.

Fadi looked around the crowded room. *Have some pride,* he berated himself. *Don't be a coward. It's not like they can beat me up in front of all these people.* Bracing himself with a deep breath and a prayer, he strode toward their table.

"Yeah, I'm Pukhtun," said Fadi. He stood straight and met Masood's probing dark eyes.

"Tough guys, those Pukhtuns," said a pudgy kid in

an oversize CAL sweatshirt. "I'm Zayd," he added with a wave.

"Uh, hi, Zayd," said Fadi.

"Take a seat," said Masood, making room next to him.

Fadi set his tray between Masood and Zayd and sat down.

"We heard you got jumped by Ike and Felix," said Masood.

Fadi nodded. His face still sported faded purplish yellow bruises.

"We also heard you gave them a dose of their own medicine," said Zayd with a huge grin.

"Those guys deserve it," mumbled a kid who was sitting across the table. His mouth was full of kebob sandwich.

"Yeah, man," piped in another boy. "Did you see Ike's busted lip?"

"They've been bossing everyone around for years," said Masood. "And now . . . now they've gotten worse."

"They're going around calling everyone a terrorist. Even the Indian and Mexican kids."

"They're, like, oppressing people, man," said the kebob sandwich eater.

Fadi nodded and carefully opened his carton of

orange juice. *"Oppressing people" is right*. He knew Felix had tried to shake Ravi down for money last week. Poor Ravi had nearly peed in his pants and passed out.

"Time for us to join forces, dudes," said Masood. He patted Fadi on the back. "Time for us to give them some of their own medicine."

Realizing he could finally get revenge, Fadi looked at the guys and smiled. "What do you have in mind?"

21
Waiting

THE PHONE RANG at four o'clock in the morning,
startling Fadi out of his sleep. "Huh?" he mumbled,
yanking the covers off of his face. The ringer sounded
again, its jagged noise filling the apartment. Before he
could even get his brain to get his body moving, footsteps pounded down the hallway.

Habib hurtled into the living room and picked up the
phone. "Hello," he said, his voice husky. In the gloom
of darkness Fadi saw a glimmer of his father's unshaven,
sleepy face. Silence descended as Habib listened to the
muffled voice on the other end. Fadi squinted through
the gloom, the hairs at the back of his neck standing up.

"Nargis *jaan*, are you sure?" said Habib. He grabbed the arm of the recliner and sat down.

Fadi blinked, all sleep gone. *What happened?* He wished he could see more clearly. He wanted to see the expression on his father's face.

"Yes, yes, that's great news," said Habib.

Fadi's heart lightened. *They've found Mariam!*

Habib sat quietly for a few minutes as *Khala* Nargis talked on the other end.

"Well, we're closer than we were last month," said Habib. His voice sounded lighter, almost happy. "I'll call you tomorrow. Zafoona will want to get all the details." After his good-byes he hung up the phone and sat as still as a stone.

Fadi pushed aside his blankets and jumped up. "What happened?" he asked. He grabbed his father's arm and shook.

"They found the family that took Mariam," said Habib.

"Where is she?" asked Fadi. His heart picked up speed as his blood gurgled through his veins.

"She wasn't with them."

"What?" His red blood cells froze. "What happened to her?"

Habib sighed and paused to collect his thoughts as

Fadi fidgeted with impatience. "Nargis tracked the family down at one of the dozens of refugee camps in Peshawar. The man, his name is Nisar, said his family had crossed over into Pakistan in the middle of September."

Right before the bombings in Jalalabad, thought Fadi.

"They paid some Pakistani soldiers to let them ride in their jeep. Once they reached Peshawar, they ended up in a refugee camp. They were given a tent, blankets, and food. But when they went to report their names at the central office, Mariam disappeared."

"What do you mean she disappeared?" whispered Fadi. Dozens of horrific scenarios played in his mind. *Was she kidnapped?*

"She ran away," said Habib. "She told the youngest son she was leaving and had him promise he wouldn't tell his parents till she was gone. She thanked them for their help, but said that she needed to find her family on her own."

"She ran away?" repeated Fadi like a silly parrot.

"Yes. When Nisar went to the office to report her missing, his wife spotted Mariam's picture on the missing person's board. She told the director that they'd brought the girl in the picture with them from Jalalabad, but that the girl had said her name was Noor, not Mariam."

"But why would she do that?"

"I don't know, *jaan*." Habib sighed. "She obviously didn't want to tell them her real name. She gave them Noor's instead."

"Yes," said Fadi. "She probably still didn't want to reveal who she was."

"The director of the refugee camp called Nargis to tell her Nisar's story and that Mariam had made it across the border."

Fadi nodded. *She's alive and she's in Peshawar,* thought Fadi with relief. He was going to find her. He knew it. Now he just needed those plane tickets.

Habib and Fadi couldn't sleep after hearing the amazing news. They sat up, eating cereal, watching old black-and-white movies until Zafoona and Noor woke up. Habib and Fadi couldn't wait to tell them the news.

"*Salaam Alaikum,*" called out Gul Khan as Habib and Fadi entered the Khyber Pass. They were meeting Uncle Amin and Zalmay there for lunch after Friday prayers.

"*Walaikum A'Salaam,* Brother Gul," said Habib. "Fadi and I had a hankering for your spicy *chapli* kebobs."

"My kebobs are at your service," said Gul Khan with a chuckle that shook his belly.

Fadi inhaled the juicy, meaty smells coming from the kitchen, and his stomach growled. His appetite had improved since he'd learned Mariam had made it to Peshawar. But now, a month and a half later, his family's relief was fading. *Khala* Nargis had men looking all over Peshawar but hadn't been able to find a single trace of her. Ever since the U.S. bombings of Jalalabad, the flood of refugees had increased tenfold, causing more confusion and chaos along the border. Fadi had hoped that by some miracle Mariam would have turned up at their aunt and uncle's clinic, but it hadn't happened. So Fadi had knelt extra long on the prayer mat at the mosque, asking Allah for Mariam's protection and for help in winning the competition.

The imam's *khutba* that week had given him hope. The topic had been the prophet Job and how his patience and devotion to Allah had persevered, no matter what calamity had befallen him—even when his body had been covered with painful sores. In the end, in reward for his patience and devotion, Allah had granted him health, family, and wealth.

According to Ms. Bethune the results of the competition had been mailed out earlier in the week, and

Fadi's nervousness was growing, despite his attempt at patience. *Think positive. With my camera skills and Anh's help, I've got to win.* He took a seat across from his father, at a table next to the window.

"Well, the talk of the town is Hamid Karzai's election," said Gul Khan, bringing them hot bread and a bowl of salad.

"It sure is," said Habib.

"Did you know that Hamid Karzai's brother has an Afghan restaurant in San Francisco?" said Gul Khan. "I bet he's going to get a lot of business after his brother's election," he added wistfully.

"*Salaam*, Gul Khan," came Uncle Amin's booming voice as he entered the restaurant.

"*Walaikum A'Salaam*," responded Gul Khan. "Sit down. The kebobs are nearly done."

Uncle Amin detoured to the bathroom while Zalmay grabbed a seat next to Fadi.

"There's talk that you're going to take on Ike and Felix," said Zalmay in a rush just as Habib stepped away to grab an Afghan newspaper.

Fadi frowned. *News sure got around.* "It's not like we want to fight them or anything," whispered Fadi. "But they keep harassing kids, so we're going to deal with them."

Zalmay's usually cheerful face was marred with worry. "I don't know, man. You don't want to make enemies out of those guys. I hear Felix's parents are some big-time lawyers with a huge office in the city."

"Oh," said Fadi. He hadn't known that.

"Yeah. They do all the legal stuff for the Filipino community."

"Quiet," shushed Fadi as Habib sat down with the paper. There was a big picture of a bearded man in a woolen Karakul hat on the cover.

"Can you believe the Afghan opposition groups actually met in Bonn, Germany, and elected a Pukhtun?" said Uncle Amin as he returned.

"Before being a Pukhtun, he's a good man," said Habib with a smile. "He was chosen by all parties in the *jirga*, including the Northern Alliance."

"That he was," said Uncle Amin. "I'm just surprised they chose him, since he supported the Taliban at one point."

"Times change. Many of us had high hopes for the Taliban," murmured Habib. "After Karzai helped throw out the Soviets, he worked with the Taliban, until they turned on him. Karzai didn't want to be their ambassador to the United Nations either."

Uncle Amin laughed. "Well, it's a tough position to fill."

Habib's smile grew broader. "True," he said wryly.

"Perhaps now we will have some peace," said Uncle Amin, his face filled with a mixture of hope and longing. "Karzai is a good man, a fair man."

"Amen to that, brother," said Gul Khan. He carried a steamer platter of kebobs and rice and plopped it down in front of them.

"Amen" is right, thought Fadi. He looked glumly at the article on Karzai's hopes for the Afghan Transitional Administration. Maybe things in Afghanistan would get better. Maybe if they had stayed there another six months, they wouldn't have had to leave. And then maybe they wouldn't have lost Mariam. Fadi sighed. That was too many maybes.

22
Results

FADI HURRIED THROUGH THE HALLS, past drooping Thanksgiving decorations, toward the art studio. The bell had just rung for lunch, and the photo club was having an all-hands meeting. Ms. Bethune had called them together after receiving notification from the contest the day before.

This is it. Today's the day. Fadi skidded around the corner, ripping the head off a paper turkey in his haste. He stopped at the entrance to the studio and paused a moment, running a hand through his rumpled hair. A glimmer of Ms. Bethune's red and silver sneakers appeared next to her desk. He hadn't slept a wink all night. All he could think about was getting on a plane with his father. In his mind he could see them flying to India, then hopping on a flight to Peshawar. *Mariam is in Peshawar, and I will find her.* Fadi took a deep breath and passed through the doors.

Ms. Bethune cleared her throat, urging everyone to settle down. "Ahem," she repeated. She pressed her lips together and fingered the large manila envelope she clutched in her left hand.

"This is it," whispered Anh.

Fadi nodded like a drunken turkey, taking his seat next to her.

Anh's eyes shined with positive energy. "Good luck, Fadi."

"You too," Fadi whispered back. His tongue was dry and stuck to the roof of his mouth, as if he'd licked an entire jar of peanut butter.

Around the room eager, nervous faces peered toward Ms. Bethune's desk. Ravi wasn't there because this type of situation made him so nervous that he usually threw up. During stressful exams he was given a seat in a corner, with a trash can, just in case. Since he couldn't be there, he'd given Fadi his phone number so someone could tell him what had happened.

"Now," said Ms. Bethune, clearing her throat, "before

I tell you the results, you must all know that you did a fantastic job, whether you won or not. The competition was stiff, with more than a thousand entries."

The huge number elicited gasps from around the room. Fadi gulped. *The chances of winning are less than a tenth of a percent.*

"Regardless of the results, we'll be going as a group to the exhibit being held at the Exploratorium in two weeks, on Saturday, so make sure to bring in your consent forms by the end of the week."

"Yeah, yeah," whispered Anh. She cracked her knuckles as her eyes narrowed. "Let's get past the pep talk and on with the show."

Fadi's gaze was glued on Ms. Bethune's hand as she slit open the envelope and pulled out a stack of pages. His heart picked up speed as she flipped past the cover page, skimming the paragraphs.

"Ahem," repeated Ms. Bethune. The sound reverberated through the silent room.

"In third place the winner is Emily Johnston, ninth grade, from Del Campo High School in Sacramento."

"Good," whispered Anh. She gave Fadi a wink. "Who wants to be in third place?"

Fadi returned a weak smile. *Third place isn't going to get me what I need.*

Ms. Bethune glanced down at the page, and her eyes widened. "In second place is . . ." Ms. Bethune looked toward Fadi, and his heart nearly stopped. "Anh Hong, sixth grade, from Brookhaven Middle School, Fremont!"

The room burst into whoops of excitement and applause.

"Way to go!" said Fadi. He turned to Anh and gave her a hug.

Anh sat with a bewildered, stunned look on her face. She was frozen, and speechless, for probably the first time in her life.

"It was that amazing action shot," said Fadi. He pounded her on the back in congratulation.

"I can't believe it," she finally whispered.

Once the ruckus died down, Ms. Bethune continued. "Awesome job, Anh. For winning second place you receive a year's free subscription to the Société Géographique magazine, free film from Kodak, and a family pass at the Exploratorium."

"Great," said Anh. "But no airline tickets," she said under her breath.

Fadi stilled. *What is the probability of two students from the same school winning? Pretty slim.* He gulped.

Ms. Bethune flipped over the page and continued.

"First place goes to Marcus Salle, seventh grade, Kifer Junior High, Belmont. Now for the grand prize . . ."

This is it, thought Fadi, saying a little prayer. *My chance to go to Peshawar.*

"The grand prize," repeated Ms. Bethune, "goes to Filbert Dewbury, eleventh grade, Calvert High School, San Jose."

What? No! Fadi's eyes widened as a cold numbness settled over his chest. *I'm supposed to win!* He gasped—he couldn't breathe.

"Fadi, are you okay?" whispered Anh. "You don't look so good."

Bile gurgled up from Fadi's stomach, making him want to throw up. His eyes closed; he slumped in his chair. He'd lost. And so had Mariam.

"Fadi . . . Fadi . . ." Anh's concerned voice flowed past him. The sounds were slow and unclear, as if people were speaking through a tunnel.

"Fadi, honey, are you okay?" Ms. Bethune hurried over.

"He's not taking this well," Fadi heard Anh respond.

"Fadi, you've been awarded an honorable mention," said Ms. Bethune. "By Clive Murray himself."

Fadi's eyes opened in surprise. "What do I win?" he said in a rush.

Ms. Bethune frowned. "It's not about winning things, Fadi."

"You don't understand," said Fadi, his voice bleak. "It is about winning. Winning those tickets to the photo shoot."

Looking confused, Ms. Bethune looked at the bottom of the page. "I'm afraid you don't win anything, Fadi," she said.

Fadi sat back as the cold numbness that had frozen his body turned into hot, boiling anger. *How could I not have won?* It was so unfair! He pounded the table with his fist and ran out of the room. He heard Ms. Bethune and Anh call after him, but he didn't care.

23
Badal

FADI RETREATED to the bathroom and locked himself in a stall for the rest of the afternoon. He pulled his legs up onto the toilet and sat as still as a statue, his mind a kaleidoscope of shock, pain, and disappointment. After an hour or so, his calves became numb and he lowered his feet to the ground. He looked at the grubby floor, strewn with toilet paper and a few pennies, and tried to think of something else—anything else.

His mind drifted to Claudia and her brother. They too had hidden in the bathroom while hiding out at the Metropolitan Museum of Art. But unlike Claudia, whose story had worked out perfectly in the end, his was a disaster.

Claudia had had her fun at the museum, had had her mystery solved by meeting Mrs. Basil E. Frankweiler, and then had headed home with her brother, safe and sound. For Fadi, things hadn't quite worked out the way he'd hoped. Neither had they for Mariam. *I've failed her again.*

A few seconds before the end-of-day bell rang, he snuck outside and wandered toward the elementary school's playground. He sat on a bench across from the jungle gym, watching a bunch of second graders hang upside down like tree sloths. A bright spot of pink caught his eye—a Hello Kitty lunch box sitting on the sidewalk. Sorrow and anger mingled, forcing him to close his eyes. After fleeing the art studio he'd wanted to take cover. He didn't want to run into Anh, or anyone else he knew, especially in the cafeteria. Now he didn't want to go home. He would have to tell Noor he'd lost—and wasted her money.

Sadness and rage bubbled through his veins, coupled with the unwelcome sense of shame. He winced, thinking back to how he'd acted like a jerk. *I can't believe I ran out of the art studio like a crybaby, and I was rude to Ms. Bethune.* But most of all, he still couldn't believe he'd lost. *All that praying and patience of Job for nothing.*

"Hey, Fadi," called out a familiar voice from across the playground.

Fadi tensed, looking for a way to avoid whoever was looking for him. He shot up from his seat, ready to duck around the corner and run back into the school, but it was too late. They'd spotted him. He watched the group of boys approach, and he blinked with annoyance.

"Hey, Fadi," shouted a nasally voice. It was Jon.

What does he want?

As the clump of boys came nearer, Fadi recognized Masood, Zayd, Ravi, and Carlos, from World History and Civilizations class. There were half a dozen other boys he didn't know.

"It's time," said Masood, his voice tense.

"Huh?" said Fadi.

"Ike and Felix are meeting Ravi at Lake Elizabeth in half an hour," said Masood. "Why?" asked Fadi.

"I told them I'd pay up this time," said Ravi. His horn-rimmed glasses sat crooked on his flushed face.

"Yeah," said Zayd. He clenched his right fist and punched his left hand. "And we're all going to be waiting for them."

A cooling salve of revenge rose up within Fadi. It was time for his *badal.* "Why didn't you tell me earlier?" he said with growing excitement.

"I called you last night, man," said Ravi. "The line was busy."

"Oh," said Fadi. Noor had been on the phone pretty much all evening.

"And you weren't at lunch," said Masood. "But no matter, we found you now. Let's go."

Fadi grabbed his backpack. "Let's go, then."

Hiding ten boys in the bushes was not easy, but somehow Fadi and the others hunkered down behind the leafy branches while Ravi stood near the designated meeting spot. It was a secluded location, tucked away in a hidden curve of a walking trail. The lake was a few feet away, home to fat frolicking ducks.

Ravi stood shivering, peering nervously at the bushes. At the crack of a twig he jumped.

"Hang in there, Ravi," whispered Fadi. He hadn't had the heart to tell him that he hadn't won anything in the Take Your Best Shot contest. Then again, neither had he.

Ravi pushed up his glasses and nodded. He stared up the path, resigned to the plan. In his hand he held a paper bag that was supposed to hold a month's worth of lunch money. In reality it was filled with marbles.

"It's three fifty-eight," whispered Masood. This was the fifth time he'd checked his watch.

"They're late," grumbled Carlos.

"As if they care about keeping Ravi waiting," said Jon. His meek demeanor had changed. He seemed unusually amped up.

"Shhh," said Fadi. He leaned forward to peer through a gap in the leaves.

Silence filtered over the spot just as Ike and Felix rounded the corner.

"Yo, Ravi," shouted Felix. "You got my money?"

Ravi gulped. "Yeah," he squeaked. He held out the crumpled bag with a shaking arm.

Fadi could hear the rattle of marbles. He tensed, going over in his mind their plan of action. As soon as Ike and Felix stood under the tree with Ravi, they were going to pounce.

"Well, what are you waiting for? Hand it over," said Ike. "I've got video games to go buy."

Ravi didn't budge. He was under strict orders to stay under the tree. It was a perfect spot for an ambush.

"I don't got all day," said Felix. He came to a halt next to Ravi and held out his hand.

Ike stopped next to him and folded his arms over his chest.

Ravi thrust the bag into Felix's hand.

"Now," spat Fadi.

Boys jumped out from all directions and surrounded the tree. They stood in a tight circle, faces set with stony expressions.

"What the . . . ," growled Ike. He and Felix backed up against the rough trunk.

Ravi smiled in relief and dove between Carlos and Jon. "We've had enough of you bossing us around," he shouted, peering over the other boys' shoulders.

"No more stealing our money, beating us up, or calling us names," said Masood, stepping forward.

"What you gonna do about it?" said Felix, straightening to his full height, which was a good six inches above Fadi.

"We're going to teach you a lesson," said Zayd.

Fadi stepped forward. "You broke my camera," he growled. The violence in his own voice startled him. But it felt good. "My father gave me that camera, and you had no right to attack me or mess with my stuff—"

"And I'm not a turban-head," interrupted Carlos. "If you're going to be a bigot, at least get it right. I'm a Mexican, man, and proud of it. But, hey, you're just a bunch of stupid bullies, so who cares what you say?"

"Yeah, man," shouted Jon. There was a hard glint in his eyes. "Who cares what you say? Ike's nothing but poor trash, pretending to be better than anyone else."

Another boy stepped forward, one Fadi didn't recognize. He looked like one of the new Samoan kids. "You may have rich parents with a fancy education," he said, pointing to Felix, "but you're just a loser who can barely read."

As the other boys laughed, Fadi joined in, a feeling of elation intoxicating him. It felt good to be the powerful one—the one who called the shots.

"Don't you dare call me that!" said Felix. He clenched his fists and stepped forward.

"Loser!" shouted the Samoan boy.

"Losers, losers, losers," chanted the boys.

Felix's face turned bright red, and he inched back toward Ike. Fear lined both boys' faces, and Fadi was thrilled. *They're getting a dose of their own medicine.*

"C'mon. Let's pound 'em," said Zayd. He sounded eager, but he looked a bit hesitant.

Fadi felt it too. It was one thing to threaten and scare the boys; it was another to actually beat them up.

"Uh, yeah," said Masood, bouncing from one foot to the other. "Let's do it."

The boys started to crowd in toward the tree.

"C'mon, you two," piped in Ravi, "try punching me." He danced in front of the boys, daring them to hit him.

As Ravi ducked away, Jon stepped forward. Fadi

frowned. Jon was struggling with something behind his back.

"Jon, no!" Fadi gasped, horrified. It was a huge fallen branch.

Masood grabbed Jon's arm as the skinny boy waved the sharp, heavy branch in front of Felix's frightened face.

"Hey, I'm just scaring him!" grumbled Jon.

"No, Jon," said Masood. He wrested the branch away from the younger boy.

Fadi's euphoria fizzled like a coal drenched in cold water. He looked from the gang of boys back to the tree, where Ike and Felix sat huddled in fear. All thoughts of revenge disintegrated. *Beating them up won't solve anything. It won't bring my camera back.* "This is getting out of hand," he said. All eyes turned toward him.

Most of the boys nodded, while Jon and Zayd shook their heads.

"We can't beat them up. That would make us as bad as they are."

"But they've been mean to us for years!" complained Zayd.

"Yeah, this is payback," grumbled Jon.

"No." Masood sighed. "Beating them up won't solve anything."

Fadi looked at each boy in turn, and they nodded their agreement.

The Samoan boy frowned. "All right," he said at last.

Fadi turned toward Ike and Felix. "Remember this. If you try to bully anyone at school again, we're going to take care of business. I suggest you really think about what you're doing."

Felix and Ike nodded with jerky movements, looking for a way out.

"Boys," called Fadi, "why don't we cool these two off so that they remember our little chat?"

Masood grinned. He along with the rest of the guys grabbed hold of Ike and Felix and threw them into the lake.

24
Confessions

ON SATURDAY MORNING THE PHOTO CLUB accompanied Ms. Bethune to the BART train station. Everyone was there, except for Ravi, whose mother thought the city was too dangerous. Bundled in a secondhand wool coat and gloves that were too big, Fadi loosened his scratchy scarf. He'd begun to feel like a lobster slowly being steamed. Ms. Bethune had warned them to dress in layers, since the San Francisco Bay Area was a patchwork of microclimates. While Fremont was a balmy sixty-five degrees in December, San Francisco, sitting next to the foggy Pacific Ocean, could be closer to thirty.

Fadi stood on the platform and peered down at the tracks. A third rail ran along the line, providing nine hundred volts of electricity to the trains. *I wouldn't want to fall on that,* he thought with a morbid shiver. He glanced over at Ms. Bethune. Her bright red lips moved as she counted heads, making sure all eleven of them were together. Her eyes landed on him, and she gave him a slow wink. Fadi smiled back, exchanging a look of understanding.

The day after he and "the brotherhood," as Fadi called them, had thrown Ike and Felix into the lake, he'd trudged the familiar path to the art studio. With roses in hand, taken from Dada's garden, he'd stood in front of Ms. Bethune's desk, his head bowed in shame.

"Ms. Bethune," he said, "I'm sorry for the way I acted yesterday."

Ms. Bethune took the flowers and pointed for him to sit across the desk. "Well, I was surprised at your reaction," she said, giving him a questioning look.

This is it. I have to tell her, thought Fadi. *I owe her the truth.* He swallowed. His tongue felt like it was coated in peanut butter. "It's just that . . . it was very important that I win the competition."

"I see," said Ms. Bethune. Her bright silver bangles

jangled as she folded her hands across the desk.

Fadi took a deep breath and told her the story of Mariam's loss. With each passing minute Ms. Bethune's face sagged and her eyes filled with tears. She kept saying "how awful" in shocked tones. At one point she reached for a sheet of felt and blew her nose.

"But that's not all of it," whispered Fadi, his own eyes bright.

"What is it, Fadi?" prodded Ms. Bethune.

A great weight shifted across Fadi's chest, constricting his lungs. He inhaled. The air caught in his throat. "You see . . . ," he began, then paused.

Ms. Bethune pursed her lips and nodded, urging him to continue.

Tell her. You've got to, thought Fadi.

Clearing his throat, he continued. "As we were running to catch the truck, Mariam was with me. She was my responsibility. She stopped. She wanted me to put her Barbie in my backpack, but we didn't have time. Suddenly the Taliban showed up. . . . We ran, but the crowd . . . There were just so many people . . . and . . . and I let go of her hand. . . . She fell."

Ms. Bethune's eyes widened.

"So you see, it's my fault she was left behind. I'm responsible."

Here it is, thought Fadi. He lowered his eyes to Ms. Bethune's long brown fingers and braced himself. *She's going to blame me.*

"Fadi," exclaimed Ms. Bethune.

Fadi looked up in surprise. She sounded sad, not angry.

Two spots of color burned on her cheeks. "You can't think that way!"

Fadi stiffened in surprise. He looked at her, his mouth open.

"It was not your fault that poor Mariam was lost."

"But . . . b-but how can you s-say that, Ms. Bethune?" stammered Fadi. "I was responsible for her. I was the one holding her hand. If I had put that stupid Barbie in my backpack, Mariam would be here."

"Look, honey," said Ms. Bethune, leaning across the desk, "bad things happen to good people. And you were in a bad, bad situation. What if you had stopped to put that darn Barbie in your bag and both of you had been left behind?"

"Oh," said Fadi. *I hadn't thought of it that way.*

"You can't second-guess yourself. It was fate that determined how things turned out."

Fadi nodded, his mind a jumble of disjointed thoughts. Maybe it wasn't fully his fault. The situation had been out of his control . . . fate, as Ms. Bethune had said.

"Now I know why those plane tickets were so important to you."

Fadi nodded. An overwhelming sense of relief flooded through his body, and he felt disjointed, like a bowl of overturned Jell-O—jiggly and without structure. Although he still felt partially responsible for Mariam's loss, he was glad he had finally told someone the truth of what had happened. As Fadi shakily got up to leave, Ms. Bethune gave him a hug.

"Now, Fadi, I have a thought," said Mrs. Bethune, tapping a burgundy fingernail on her chin. "Why don't we have a fund-raiser for you?"

At Fadi's confused look, she continued. "We can collect money for a plane ticket to Peshawar."

"Can we really do that?" asked Fadi, a hope flaring in his chest.

"I don't see why not. We have collection jars, car washes, bingo nights, all sorts of fund-raisers at the school for different causes. I think the students and faculty would love to pitch in and help find Mariam."

With a dazed smile Fadi thanked Ms. Bethune and headed home, a new spring in his step.

Fadi later shared the idea with Anh, and she thought it was brilliant. Her new project was to take on the

Bring Mariam Home campaign. It might take months of bake sales and car washes, but maybe, just maybe, they could raise the money. One ticket for Habib. Fadi knew that it should be his father who brought Mariam home. Fadi would do his part to raise the money, but his father had to be the one who found her. Then both would have their honor restored. As he walked home after school, there was an ease to his step that had been missing for months, but guilt still ate at his conscience. He had to tell his family—tell them it wasn't their fault Mariam was lost.

A series of loud beeps interrupted his thoughts, announcing an oncoming train, along with the flashing electronic destination sign announcing OAKLAND–SAN FRANCISCO. Fadi stepped back as the silver train pulled into the station, sending a burst of wind whipping through his hair. Anh's patent leather shoes shone in the sun as she practically skipped through the doorway. Fadi trudged behind, and they grabbed seats next to the window. With a resigned sigh Fadi watched Fremont zip by.

"This'll be fun. You'll see," said Anh. She passed Fadi a piece of licorice from the stock of candy she'd packed for the trip.

Fadi took it and stuck it into his mouth. "If you say so," he mumbled between chews. He hadn't wanted to go, but Anh had nagged him every day till he'd gotten his father to sign his consent form. He'd realized that if he acted like a sore loser, he wouldn't be able to celebrate Anh's victory. As the spicy flavor of anise spread over his taste buds, his mind floated back to his conversation with his father earlier in the week.

With dinner over, Zafoona and Noor had gone to visit *Khala* Nilufer, but Fadi had stayed, using the excuse that he had too much math homework. As raindrops beat against the window, Fadi and his father put together a snack for themselves in the warm comfort of the kitchen. For Fadi it was his usual, a sliced Twinkie spread with peanut butter and layered with a sliced banana. Habib took a handful of sugared almonds and made a pot of green tea. As Fadi pulled a carton of milk from the fridge, he contemplated the best way to break the news to his father. He watched the pearly froth reach the rim of his glass, and took a deep breath.

Just do it, he ordered. So he opened his mouth. "Dad . . . ," he began. "I found out that . . . that I didn't win the photography competition."

"Oh," said Habib. He glanced over with a commiserating frown. "Well, you tried your best."

But my best wasn't good enough, thought Fadi with a dull ache in his chest. "But, Dad," said Fadi, "you don't understand. I wasted fifty dollars and didn't win the tickets to India."

Habib chewed thoughtfully on an almond and pulled a volume of Rumi's poetry from a row of books next to the microwave. "Tell me one thing," he said. "Did you enjoy taking those pictures—did you learn anything?"

Fadi looked at his father's untroubled expression and paused in confusion. He recalled the thrill that had coursed through him when he'd spent the day in San Francisco with Habib, walking up and down Fillmore Street. It had been a blast working with Anh, Abay, and Dada on his second group of pictures. He'd also finally gotten the hang of taking pictures at dusk, which was really tricky. "Sure, I enjoyed it—and I learned something new."

"Well, that's the most important thing," said Habib. "Winning isn't everything, Fadi *jaan*. As Rumi says, 'When you do things from your soul, you feel a river moving in you, a joy.' So, Fadi, you must do things that you love. You never know what rewards may come of it."

Fadi sighed at his father's philosophizing. *But, Dad, in this case winning was everything,* he thought. He gathered the nerve to tell his father something else . . . tell him about his role in Mariam's loss, but the teakettle whistled, and as Habib turned away, Fadi lost his nerve.

Even Noor hadn't batted an eyelash when he'd told her, earlier in the day, that he'd wasted her money. "Hey, kid, you tried," she'd said. With a toss of her hair, she'd run out to work before he could bring up Mariam.

Why do they have to be so understanding? They should have gotten pissed off at me, told me I was a loser. It's because they don't know it was me who lost Mariam. And now I've lost yet another chance to find her.

Fadi looked out the train window, and something stiffened inside him. *I have to come clean.* He'd been hiding the truth for too long, and it was rusting away his insides. Telling Ms. Bethune had been good, but he had to tell his family. Resolve crystallized within him. *Where is my sense of honor?* He sat up taller and straightened his spine. *I'm going to tell Father, Mother, and Noor it was my fault— it was me who lost Mariam.* When the family sat down around the table that night, he was going to tell them what had really happened, and finally take responsibility for Mariam's loss.

Exploratorium

WITH THOUGHTS OF FINALLY REVEALING the truth to his family whirling through his mind, Fadi felt the train slow as it entered West Oakland station, the last stop in the East Bay before entering the city. After picking up additional passengers, the train slipped into a tunnel that angled downward. For a moment the lights flickered and the passengers were plunged into darkness. Fadi gripped his seat, feeling a little claustrophobic. The lights flickered back on and the train shot forward.

Oooh, I think I'm going to be sick, thought Fadi, glancing upward. There were a gazillion tons of water sloshing overhead.

"It's okay, Fadi," whispered Anh. She patted his hand. "Think about it. It's like our art project—*Twenty Thousand Leagues Under the Sea*. We're on the submarine, the *Nautilus*."

Fadi gave a dry chuckle, the tension in his body easing a bit. Within minutes the train popped up on dry land and slowed into Embarcadero Station. From there Ms. Bethune guided her charges to the Muni stop, where they caught the number four tram to the Marina District.

"I just love the city," breathed Anh. With her nose pressed against the window, she soaked up the action outside.

The city was beautiful, decked out for the holidays. Bright colored lights sparkled from the trees, while storefronts competed with one another to be the most festive with their decorations.

"It's too crowded for me," said Fadi. He eyed the throngs of shoppers marching down the sidewalk, arms overflowing with packages. "I need green open spaces."

"But there's so much happening," said Anh. "So many things to see, to do, and to eat."

"The weather's too wacky," said Fadi. He eyed the fog, which still sat in a thick layer atop the Bank of America building, blocking out the sun. Back in Oakland the sun had been shining.

They bickered amicably about the merits of living in the city until the tram stopped and Ms. Bethune herded them off.

"See," said Anh. "Green spaces."

"Wow," breathed Fadi. He stepped down from the bottom step and blinked in surprise. Across the street stood a majestic domed Greek temple, situated on the banks of a winding shallow lagoon. Swans moved gracefully through the reeds, past rosy stone columns.

"Ta-da," said Anh. "The Palace of Fine Arts."

"It's awesome," said Fadi. He retied his scarf against the chill and followed the group along Palace Drive. The entrance to the museum was at the rear of the Palace of Fine Arts, on Lyons Street, two blocks up.

The colorful sign announcing the Exploratorium hung over a series of tall oval doors. Ms. Bethune collected the group at the entrance and handed them their tickets and name tags.

Fadi stuck his tag on his chest as Anh pointed to a plaque on the ground. It read FOUNDED IN 1969 BY THE PHYSICIST DR. FRANK OPPENHEIMER.

"Totally brilliant man," said Anh. "He and his brother worked on a top secret project to make the atom bomb during World War II."

Man, she is so Claudia, thought Fadi with a grin.

"Come along, gang," said Ms. Bethune with a wide smile. They skipped through a set of glass doors and headed past the information booth to the vast foyer inside.

Wow, thought Fadi. It was the largest room he'd ever been in—well, besides the arrival hall at the San Francisco airport. Arrows directed guests to hundreds of hands-on scientific exhibits. A large sign stood at the center announcing the photography competition and exhibit. Fadi followed Ms. Bethune and the others through the cavernous space until they reached the exhibition hall. He stepped inside and eyed dozens of huge photographs set up on easels. Other pictures hung from the ceiling or were mounted on boards. Hundreds of kids milled around, talking, laughing, and inspecting the winning entries.

"Okay, guys, we'll meet in half an hour, at that column over there," said Ms. Bethune, pointing to the right corner. "We'll go to the awards ceremony together in the next room. After refreshments we'll head home at two o'clock. So scoot—go and have fun. Now, Anh, I believe you have to report to the judges."

"Okay," said Anh. She turned to Fadi. "I'll find out what they want and come look for you."

"No problem," said Fadi. He watched as she rushed

over to the reception table. San Francisco City Councilman Henry Watson shook her hand as she fidgeted in excitement. Though Fadi was happy for her, he couldn't help but feel a little bit envious. He loosened his scarf and pulled off his mittens, which he stuffed into his coat pocket. Alone, he wandered over to the winners' circle. He checked out Anh's shot. It was huge, nearly four feet by six. Her name and school were written at the bottom.

You could see every detail of the dancers in motion. He was struck again by the emotion radiating off the paper. He circled left to the third-place winner. Emily Johnston had taken a picture of a tiny kitten sitting on top of a Saint Bernard's head. The shot was cropped well—the Saint Bernard's eyes looked up while the kitten looked down, drawing the viewer's eyes to the expressions on their faces. *Cute, but predictable.*

He crossed back to see the first-place photo by Marcus Salle. He'd taken a picture of an ancient redwood tree standing solemnly against the backdrop of the Pacific Ocean. *Cool.* Fadi peered closely at the tree's winding roots pushing up from the rich soil. You could almost smell the salty air coming off the waves. *Very cool. But a first-place winner? I don't know. But heck, I'm not the judge.*

The grand prize winner, Filbert Dewbury from Calvert High School, stood as proud as a peacock next to his winning shot. Every so often he straightened his bow tie and grinned with perfect pearl white teeth.

"Congratulations," said Fadi.

"Thanks," said Filbert, puffing out his chest.

Fadi moved away as a group of girls approached them. He stood next to the winning picture and whistled in appreciation. He could see why it had been chosen. A creative action shot, it showed a skydiver falling backward into a wide expanse of crystalline sky. You could see the plane's door, which created a really cool 3-D effect. The expression on the skydiver's face was really funny. All elements were there—simplicity, composition, and lighting.

Don't be a sore loser, he reminded himself, and moved on, toward a line of photographs on the side wall. The sign above the board read TOP FIFTY SHOTS. *Nice,* he thought, starting at the top. There were amazing pictures, some silly, some serious, some sad and intense. At the bottom left-hand corner he spotted Dada handing Abay a rose, and his pulse quickened. He bent closer to see the soft shadows created by the hazy light at dusk.

At least I made it into the top fifty.

"That was one of my favorites," said a deep voice behind him.

Fadi jumped in surprise and turned around.

"Sorry. Didn't mean to startle you," said the gray-mustached man. He wore a faded tweed jacket and jeans.

Fadi recognized him from his picture. It was Clive Murray.

"Uh . . . hello," said Fadi with a gulp. "Mr. Murray."

"Call me Clive," he said with a smile. He looked at Fadi's badge. "So you're Fadi, huh?"

"Uh . . . yes," said Fadi.

"Well, I really like the way you've framed the shot. You can see that the subjects don't even know they're being photographed."

"Thanks," said Fadi, his insides warming.

"Personally, I love portrait shots. Wherever I am, even in the turbulent war zones or battlefields, I always stop to take pictures of people. People's faces reveal the real story to me."

"It wasn't easy," said Fadi. "The lighting was a challenge."

"Lighting can be your friend or foe." Clive chuckled.

Fadi nodded. "Especially dusk."

"You should keep practicing and take some risks,"

said Clive. "Making mistakes will help you learn. I still make mistakes to this day."

"Really?" said Fadi. He couldn't imagine Clive making mistakes.

"C'mon. I'll show you. I put together some stuff for you kids to look at—to learn from."

Fadi followed Clive to a table in the back. A Société Géographique banner stretched along the front.

"Those are some of my latest pictures from my last trip to Africa and Asia," said Clive, pointing to a large album. "Now let me look for that humdinger of a shot where I cut someone's head off!"

Fadi smiled and flipped open the album. The first picture showed a group of women wading through a rice paddy as bombs went off in the distant mountains. *You have to eat, even during war,* thought Fadi sadly. The next picture revealed a militia group carrying machetes, marching down the road in some dusty African country. Fadi blinked in surprise at the next shot: a young man wearing a black turban standing with a rifle. The photo next to it was of a group of women in stained blue burkas, walking along a dirt road. "Where were these taken?" asked Fadi, his voice soft.

"Along the Pakistan-Afghan border," said Clive. "I was covering the recent outbreak of fighting there."

"Oh," said Fadi, his voice subdued. He turned the page. His eyes widened, and his breath froze in his lungs. The picture showed a refugee camp. Transfixed, he stared down at the group of children playing, framed by a group of tents. One of the girls clutched a doll wearing a stained and torn hot pink burka.

Epilogue

NO ONE HAD TO FLY to Peshawar to get Mariam.
With Clive Murray's help she was tracked down to the
refugee camp where he'd taken the picture. That night
Habib called the American consulate and *Khala* Nargis
and told them where to find Mariam. Within twenty-four
hours she was picked up and was on board a flight to San
Francisco, courtesy of the American Consulate General.
Two days later, the entire family—minus Abay and
Dada—huddled together at San Francisco International
Airport, waiting outside customs. Habib carried flowers,
while helium-filled balloons bobbed above Uncle Amin's
head. Zalmay and all the cousins held welcome signs as

Noor kept them in line. *Khala* Nilufer and Zafoona hovered closest to the doors, clasping each other's hands. Fadi stood off to the side, his backpack slung over his shoulder. Inside rested the rusty old honey tin, three new Barbies, and a box of extra fancy chocolates. His eyes were glued to the doorway, his breath catching in his throat whenever a passenger came through. Then, there it was—a flash of pink. Mariam bounced through the doors, accompanied by a customs official. As if tracking Fadi with her inner radar, she paused. Within seconds her hazel eyes discovered his and she ran, intercepted by Habib's bear hug and their mother's happy sobs.

That night, at the boisterous celebratory dinner at Uncle Amin's house, Fadi ate an entire plateful of *mantu*, savoring every bite. Gulmina, a little battered from her recent experiences, sat in a place of honor, between him and Mariam. Fadi glanced at his sister's profile, animated by the tale of how she'd made it across the border into Peshawar. She'd lost weight and her face was thinner, but it was *her*. His fingers crept across the soft carpeted floor, behind Gulmina's back. He folded Mariam's hand into his and squeezed. Mariam glanced back at him and grinned, then launched back into her story. As her small fingers rested in his palm, a warm, satisfied fullness settled through Fadi's body.

Glossary

Alhamdulillah—Arabic phrase meaning "Praise to God" or "All praise belongs to God." In everyday speech it simply means "Thank God!" It is used by Muslims and also by Arabic-speaking Jews and Christians.

ameen—Means "amen" in Arabic.

bacha—Means "child" in Pukhto and Farsi. "Bachay" is plural, for "children."

badal—Code of blood feuds or revenge in Pukhtunwali.

burka—Enveloping outer garment worn by women in some Islamic countries.

chapli kebob—A popular dish among Pukhtuns in Afghanistan and Pakistan made from spiced minced beef or lamb, cooked on a large flat griddle.

charg—Means "chicken" in Pukhto and Persian.

dastarkhan—Tablecloth laid out on the ground for family meals, which are traditionally eaten on the floor.

dogh—Drink made of yogurt and water, and can also have cucumber and herbs.

Farsi—Persian language spoken in Afghanistan (also called Dari).

ghayrat—Sense of honor and pride in Pukhtunwali.

Hazara—Persian-speaking group, 9 percent of Afghanistan's population.

hofbrau—German brewery, bar, and restaurant.

imam—Prayer leader of a mosque.

insha'Allah—Expression meaning "if God wills," used to suggest that something in the future is uncertain.

jaan—Means "love" or "dearest" in Pukhto and Persian.

Jalalabad—City in eastern Afghanistan, near the Pakistan border.

loya jirga—Pukhto term that means "grand council." A *loya jirga* is a political meeting usually used to choose new kings, adopt constitutions, or decide important political matters and disputes.

kebob—Variety of meat dishes consisting of grilled or broiled meats on a skewer or stick.

Kabul—Capital of Afghanistan, and largest city in Afghanistan.

Karakul cap—Hat made from the fleece of the Karakul sheep. Typically worn by Muslim men in Central and South Asia.

KGB, or Komitet Gosudarstvennoi Bezopasnosti—National security umbrella organization of the Soviet Union that also had operations in Afghanistan during the Soviet invasion.

khala—Means "aunt" in Pukhto.

khutba—Religious sermon given at weekly Friday prayers.

mantu—Steamed ravioli-type dumplings filled with spiced meat, served with a meat, lentil, and yogurt sauce.

mashallah—Literally means "Whatever Allah (God) wills." It is often used on occasions when there is surprise in someone's good deeds or achievements.

melmastia—Code of hospitality and protection to every guest in Pukhtunwali.

mihrab—Niche in the wall of a mosque that indicates the *qibla*—that is, the direction of the Kaaba in Mecca—and hence the direction that Muslims should face when praying.

namus—Concept of family, and particularly the protection of women, in Pukhtunwali.

Northern Alliance—Military-political umbrella organization created in 1996. The organization united various competing non-Pukhtun Afghan groups to fight the Taliban.

panah—Concept of asylum in Pukhtunwali.

Peshawar—Capital of the North-West Frontier Province of Pakistan.

Pukhtuns—Largest ethnic group in Afghanistan, composing 42 percent of the population. They speak Pukhto.

Pukhto—Indo-European language spoken primarily by the Pukhtuns.

Pukhtunwali—Concept of living, or philosophy, for the Pukhtun people. It is regarded as an honor code and unwritten law.

pulao—Dish of rice that contains a variety of meats and vegetables.

qabuli pulao—Fragrant rice pulao made with lamb and covered with candied carrots and raisins.

Qur'an—Central religious text of Islam. Muslims believe the Holy Qur'an is the book of divine guidance and direction for mankind, and they consider the original Arabic text to be the final revelation of God.

Taliban—Means "student." It was a predominately Pukhtun movement that governed Afghanistan from 1996 until 2001.

Salaam Alaikum—Means "Peace be upon you." Arabic greeting used by Muslims as well as Arab Christians and Jews.

surah—A "chapter" of the Holy Qur'an.

Tajik—Persian-speaking people and the second largest ethnic group in Afghanistan, with 27 percent of the population.

taqueria—Spanish word for a taco shop.

Uzbek—Persian-speaking ethnic group; 9 percent of Afghanistan's population.

Walaikum A'Salaam—Means "and upon you be peace." The traditional response to "Salaam Alaikum."

Author's Note

I DIDN'T WANT TO WRITE THIS BOOK . . . really, I didn't. I resisted it for many years. Why? Because it deals with many sensitive and personal issues—9-11, the war on terror, Islam, Afghan culture and politics, coupled with my husband's family history and escape from Kabul, Afghanistan. But no matter how hard I tried to ignore it, the story kept niggling the back of my mind. So finally, I was compelled to tell it. After much thought I decided to write a fictionalized account of my husband's story while explaining the complexities and nuances of Afghan culture and politics in a way that could be understood by young and old alike.

My husband's father was a professor at Kabul University in the late 1970s. Like Fadi's father, he too received a PhD in agriculture from the University of Wisconsin, Madison. When the Soviets invaded Afghanistan in 1979 and supplanted a communist puppet government, intellectuals like him were forced to make a decision: join the regime, go to prison and be tortured, or flee the country. Like my husband's father, Fadi's father was forced to make a similar decision. Although their escapes occurred at different times and took different routes, both embarked on a perilous journey that brought them to the United States. My husband fled with his parents and younger brother, who, unlike Mariam, was not accidentally left behind. Similarly, both families dealt with the trials and tribulations of adjusting to a new life in the United States. My husband, like Fadi, grew up and adjusted to life in America as a refugee and dealt with new schools, bullies, and discrimination—but both adjusted, made friends, pursued their dreams, and flourished.

For thousands of years, Afghanistan has been a battleground for outsiders. Alexander the Great and Genghis Khan came with their armies, as did the British and the Soviets. All attempted to conquer and occupy, yet failed. There are lessons to be learned as the United

States currently contemplates its role in this war-torn country. It is a land still ravaged by war and ethnic tensions between various groups—Pukhtun, Tajik, Hazara, Uzbek, and others. Despite these facts, Afghans remain a strong and proud people.

Shooting Kabul ends on a hopeful note with the election of President Karzai. By the end of 2001 the Taliban had been forced to the fringes of the country and a new hope had reawakened in the country. Unfortunately, nearly a decade later, the Taliban have surged again. The government in Kabul today, under Karzai, with U.S. backing, continues to emphasize a central government in Kabul while neglecting the rest of the country. This does not bode well for Afghans who want nothing more than the basic necessities—clean water, employment, education, and security. It saddens me that Afghanistan is yet again at a crossroads, with its people caught at the center of indecision and conflict. They are a people with a resilient and long history, desiring peace for their children and respect from the outside world. But I, like others, still have hope—hope that peace, security, and prosperity will come, *insha'*Allah.

Further Reading

Books

Ali, Sharifah Enayat. *Afghanistan (Cultures of the World)*. New York: Benchmark Books, 2006.

Armstrong, Jennifer. *Shattered: Stories of Children and War*. New York: Laurel-Leaf, 2003.

Banting, Erinn. *Afghanistan: The Land (Lands, Peoples, and Cultures)*. New York: Crabtree Publishing, 2003.

Clements, Andrew. *Extra Credit*. New York: Atheneum, 2009.

Ellis, Deborah. *The Breadwinner*. Toronto: Groundwood Books, 2001.

————. *Mud City*. Toronto: Groundwood Books, 2004.

————. *Parvana's Journey*. Toronto: Groundwood Books, 2003.

Khan, Rukhsana. *Wanting Mor*. Toronto: Groundwood Books, 2009

Mortenson, Greg. *Three Cups of Tea: One Man's Journey to Change the World . . . One Child at a Time (The Young Reader's Edition)*. New York: Puffin, 2009.

O'Brien, Tony, and Mike Sullivan. *Afghan Dreams: Young Voices of Afghanistan*. New York: Bloomsbury USA Children's Books, 2008.

Reedy, Trent. *Words in the Dust*. New York: Arthur A. Levine Books, 2011.

Staples, Suzanne Fisher. *Under the Persimmon Tree*. New York: Square Fish, 2008.

Weber, Valerie J. *I Come from Afghanistan (This Is My Story)*. Pleasantville, NY: Weekly Reader Early Learning Library, 2006.

Whitfield, Susan. *National Geographic Countries of the World: Afghanistan*. Des Moines: National Geographic Children's Books, 2008.

Websites

CIA WORLD FACTBOOK
https://www.cia.gov/library/publications/the-world-factbook/geos/af.html

BBC NEWS COUNTRY PROFILE: AFGHANISTAN
http://news.bbc.co.uk/2/hi/south_asia/country_profiles/1162668.stm

NATIONAL GEOGRAPHIC
http://travel.nationalgeographic.com/places/countries/country_afghanistan.html

OXFAM'S COOL PLANET: AFGHANISTAN
http://www.oxfam.org.uk/coolplanet/kidsweb/world/afghan/index.htm

WORLD ATLAS
http://www.worldatlas.com/webimage/countrys/asia/af.htm

Reading Guide to
Shooting
KABUL

BY N. H. SENZAI

ABOUT THIS GUIDE

The discussion questions and activities that follow are intended to enhance your reading of *Shooting Kabul*. Please feel free to adapt these materials to suit the needs of your classroom or community group.

DISCUSSION QUESTIONS

1. Chapter 1 begins with the sentence, "It's a perfect night to run away . . ." From what is the family running at the opening of the story? Describe at least three ways in which running away (or choosing to stay) is an important idea in terms of the novel's plot and themes.

2. Describe the main character, Fadi. What are his interests and dreams? What roles does he play within both his immediate family and his larger Afghan community in California? How are Fadi's family and community relationships similar to, or different from, your own?

3. Why did Fadi's father, Habib, choose to return to Afghanistan? What does this choice tell you about Habib? If you were a member of Habib's family, how would you have felt about this decision?

4. What happens to Fadi's sister, Mariam, as the family embarks on their escape from Afghanistan? How are feelings of guilt and responsibility about this incident expressed differently by various members of the family?

5. What do Fadi's memories of life with Mariam teach readers about Afghanistan? What type of doll is Gulmina? Is this important? In what ways might this doll be viewed as a symbol of the west? Can you think of other ideas represented by Gulmina?

6. How does Fadi react to meeting his extended family in San Francisco? How does Mariam's absence affect this reunion? In what ways do family members reach out to Fadi, Noor, and their parents? What is life like in Uncle Amin's house? What job does Habib take in America?

7. At his new school, Fadi ". . . felt as though he were hidden behind a camera lens, watching another world whirl past in shattered fragments." (p. 84) What does this observation tell you about Fadi's adaptation to his new school? Is he able to form friendships? What kinds of groups does he encounter at school?

8. What happens to Fadi's camera? What does Fadi's behavior after the fight with Felix teach you about Fadi? Who helps Fadi enter the photography contest anyway? What is the first picture Fadi takes for the contest? Why does he reject this picture as his contest entry?

9. How does Fadi discover the real picture he wants to take? What brings him to this decision? Have you ever entered a creative or athletic contest? What were your hopes for the outcome? How are they similar to, or different from, Fadi's reasons for wanting to win?

10. Does Fadi win the contest? How does the contest experience help the family find Mariam? Once Mariam gets to America, do you think Fadi and the others are able to let go of their guilt? Explain your answer.

11. How does the author interweave real world events with the fictional story of Fadi and his family? How do the events of September 11, 2001, affect Fadi's school and home life? What types of misunderstandings about the Muslim faith and Middle Easterners more generally are shown in the novel? What has the novel taught you about Afghan culture?

12. Why is this novel entitled "Shooting Kabul"? Were you surprised, when you reached the end of the story, at the meaning of "shooting" that the author wanted to convey? After finishing the novel and reading the subsequent Author's Note, what do you feel is the most important idea or message of this story?

WRITING & RESEARCH ACTIVITIES

I. Through the Lens

1. Write a short essay describing what photograph you would choose enter a "Take Your Best Shot" contest. If possible, take some pictures. Choose your best shot and write a brief explanation of why you like your selection. With friends or classmates, create a photography display.

2. The author uses the camera, and photography-related words and images, to help readers better understand Fadi's experiences. Include photography-related language to write a journal entry describing an experience in your own life.

3. Go to your local library or bookstore and look through books by famous photographers such as Ansel Adams, Dorothea Lange, and Alfred Stieglitz. Select a photograph that is particularly thought-provoking or inspiring to you. Write a short essay describing the photograph and your thoughts.

4. Go to the library or online to find a picture of Fadi's old camera, the Minolta XE. Write a short paragraph explaining the history of this camera. Then research cameras and photography to choose a camera you would like to use if you were entering a photography contest. Write a brief description of this camera.

II. Beyond the Book

1. Read Fadi's favorite book, *From the Mixed-up Files of Mrs. Basil E. Frankweiler* by E. L. Konigsburg. Then write a two- to three-page essay explaining why you think this book is so meaningful to Fadi.

2. Do you have a favorite book that you read again and again? Create a poster featuring this book. Include a summary of the plot, a list of main characters, and illustrations of the cover or other important images. Present your poster to friends or classmates, making sure to explain why this book is special to you.

3. Both *Shooting Kabul* and *From the Mixed-up Files of Mrs. Basil E. Frankweiler* feature works of art. N. H. Senzai includes the work of fictional photographer Clive Murray. E. L. Konigsburg's mystery involves the art of Michelangelo. Using what you have learned from reading these novels, write an essay explaining how art and literature can help young people learn more about themselves.

4. Running away is an important concept in both novels. Create a poem, song lyrics, drawing, story, or other creative work exploring the idea of running away.

ABOUT ANOTHER WORLD

1. Afghanistan is a country with a rich history. Create an illustrated time line of at least twenty notable moments in Afghan history beginning as far back as 500 B.C.

2. In her Author's Note, N. H. Senzai tells readers that she "didn't want to write this book." Write a letter to the author explaining why you are thankful she did write *Shooting Kabul* after all.

3. Go to the library or online to find a map of modern-day Afghanistan. Learn more about the various ethnic groups that live in this country, including Pukhtun, Tajik, Hazara, and Uzbek. Research the Taliban and the effect this organization has had on Afghanistan. Find a newspaper article less than two weeks old that provides information on the current situation in Afghanistan. Imagine you are an advisor to the American president. Present information from your research to help the president better understand the situation in Afghanistan.

4. Go to the library or online to find a recipe for *mantu*. With adult help, prepare this dish for friends or classmates. Invite friends or classmates to share favorite ethnic recipes enjoyed by their families. Create a class cookbook, including recipes and short paragraphs in which each student explains the origin or importance of the recipe they shared.

Acknowledgments

I'd like to thank all the people without whose guidance and support this book would not be a reality. First, my elementary school librarians, Carolyn Hackworth and Becky Murray, who taught me the mysteries of the Dewey decimal system and instilled a passion for the written word. To the teachers at Jubail Academy, who always told me I could be whatever I wanted, especially Jo Cochran, who sparked the desire to string words into stories in her Novel Writing Club—your encouragement was the spark every student needs. Also, *gracias* to Dan Yurkovich, whose photo club taught me all about enlargers and zoom lenses. Thanks to my critique partners, Doug Marshall and Alexis Whaley, who whipped my manuscript into shape and cheered me on. Much gratitude and appreciation to Michael Bourret, my astute and savvy agent at Dystel and Goderich Literary Agency, and the über-talented team at Simon & Schuster, orchestrated by my clever and insightful editor, Alexandra Penfold. Much admiration to Yan Nascimbene, who distilled the essence of *Shooting Kabul* within his extraordinary artwork. And last but not least, to my parents, Mon, and sisters—Shahla and Farah—and my inspiring and rambunctious nieces and nephews, Omar, Hasan, Noor, Mariam, and Ali.

Are you longing to know what happens?
Check out N. H. Senzai's next book,

Saving Kabul Corner!

ARIANA HAPHAZARDLY SHOVELED PISTACHIOS into a bin and tried not to glare at her cousin, Laila, who knelt near the cash register, carefully stacking jars of cherry jam. Laila's long-lashed aquamarine eyes glowed with concentration, and a thoughtful frown marred her face, which was framed with silky brown hair roped together in a neat braid. After finishing her task quickly and efficiently, Laila floated down the aisle toward a stack of boxes that had just been delivered. She wasn't stampeding like a rhino, which Ariana had often been told she resembled. Ariana could just imagine her mother's voice ringing in her ears.

Ariana jaan, please try to be more ladylike. . . . Walk, don't gallop. . . . Watching Laila glide down the checkered linoleum floor, Ariana fumed. *She really is perfect.*

Nearly thirteen, Laila could cook like a proper Afghan girl, as well as sew, embroider, recite classical poetry, and sing in three languages—Pukhto, Farsi, and English. She'd also been the top student at her all-girls school back in Kabul. Only a few months younger, Ariana could barely toast a Pop-Tart without burning it, or sew a button on a shirt without pricking her finger on the needle. As Ariana surreptitiously watched Laila, she tried to squash the hot, throbbing sensation blossoming near her heart. She couldn't help it. *I hate her guts. Which are probably also perfect.*

With a dejected sigh Ariana glowered at the pistachios that had escaped the bin, a hint of guilt blossoming in her heart. Laila was her cousin, and it wasn't Laila's fault that she was, well, *perfect.* But ever since Laila had arrived and moved into their tiny town house with them on Peralta Boulevard a month ago, things had changed drastically for Ariana. While Laila's mother had taken Ariana's eldest brother, Zayd's, bedroom, Laila had moved into Ariana's postage-stamp-size space that she'd already been sharing with their grandmother Hava Bibi. Laila's father was Hava

Bibi's nephew and part of the huge Shinwari clan from which they got their last name. Since Hava Bibi was an elder within a close-knit Afghan family, she was considered to be Laila's grandmother too. The moment Laila and her mother had touched down in San Francisco, their extended family had flown into a frenzy of activity. Every other day there had been a party, welcoming them to their new life in the United States, away from war-torn Afghanistan. Ariana felt like an extra shoe, lying around, trying to find the right foot to fit.

With a muffled sigh Ariana looked away, trying to think of something, anything, to squelch the flood of negative thoughts. Then it flashed before her, the date she'd circled in red on her Peanuts calendar back home—January 27, one hundred and forty-seven days away. That day represented something that she'd hungered for for as long as she could remember—*privacy*. During spring break her parents had taken her and her three brothers down to a new subdivision at the foot of Mission Hills. After touring the model homes, her father, Jamil, had put a down payment on a two-story white stucco house with a red tiled roof. It was their dream house, which they'd been saving up for four years, and her dad made sure there was something for everyone: a modern kitchen with modern steel appliances for her mother, and a huge family room with a brand-new wide screen television so Hava Bibi could watch her Afghan soaps. A spacious backyard jutted out behind the house, and best of all, there was a separate bedroom for each of the four kids. Ariana recalled the blueprints, printed on soft turquoise paper, where her father had pointed out her very own bedroom, overlooking the green hills beyond.

"Hey," grumbled Zayd, interrupting Ariana's daydream. At seventeen he'd appointed himself third in command, after their father and their father's younger brother Uncle Shams, co-owners of the family grocery store, Kabul Corner. "Who's going to eat *those*?" he asked, glaring at the stray nuts on the floor. "Do you think money grows on trees or something?"

Thankfully, she didn't have to answer, because their nine-year-old twin brothers, Omar and Hasan, teetered by, lugging a fifty-pound bag of flour between them.

"Man, can you lift higher?" complained Omar. He was younger than Hasan by two minutes.

"Dude, I'm doing the best I can," grumbled Hasan, his skinny arms trembling.

In their haste to reach the bakery at the back of the

store, they crashed into a shelf, sending a line of cans thudding to the floor.

"Watch it, you two!" yelled Zayd, running toward them.

Laila came running around the corner, carrying an unwieldy box, her head barely visible behind it. "I'll help them," she said. Laila set down the box and grabbed one end of the bag. "Come on, I know you have the muscles, but I'm going to help you navigate to the bakery."

"Thanks," chorused the twins, following her lead.

"Ari!" shouted Zayd, using her nickname, his arms full of cans. "Get with it! The store's about to open. Help Laila with that box."

Before Ariana could get up off the floor, Laila returned to move the box of cashews herself. She avoided Ariana's gaze and focused on reaching the nut bins.

"Thanks for being so helpful around the store," said Zayd, smiling at Laila, then shooting Ariana an irritated look.

"It's no problem," said Laila, giving Zayd a tentative smile. "I like helping out."

"You're totally awesome," said Zayd, ruffling her hair and handing her a scoop.

Steamed at the love fest, Ariana fled to the front of the store, leaving Laila to fill the cashew bin with *perfect* precision, not dropping a single nut. Ariana paused a moment to run her hand along a display of embroidered cushions, letting the soft maroon velvet soothe her fingertips. All around the store she could see the hard work her father and uncle had put in. It was their pride and joy. When Kabul Corner had opened its doors nearly a decade before, it had been the first large Afghan grocery store in the city. With a prime location in central Fremont, the hub of the Afghan community, the store had quickly become *the* place to find spices; freshly baked bread; halal meat, slaughtered according to Islamic regulations; and a good gossip session. She sniffed the warm, sweet scent of cinnamon, mixed in with the earthy smell of cumin, and knelt beside the spice rack to organize it, just as her uncle walked through the door.

"*Salaam alaikum*, Uncle Shams," said Ariana.

"*Walaikum a'salaam, jaan*," said Uncle Shams, narrowing his eyes at the stack of spice packets. "Make sure those are hung properly. Last time, you mixed the cayenne pepper in with the cinnamon. Mrs. Balkh accidently bought the wrong thing and complained to me about it for a week."

"Yes, Uncle Shams," muttered Ariana, ducking away.

"*Salaam,*" Uncle Shams greeted Jamil.

"*Walaikum a'salaam,*" replied Jamil, who was organizing the cash register.

This was the final countdown. Thirty minutes until opening, and there was still a lot of work to do.

"I'm glad you got more flour," said Jamil. "We were running out."

"I picked it up at Costco," said Uncle Shams, angling his rotund body through the gap to slip behind the counter. He was short and round, in contrast to Ariana's father, who was lanky and slim. People sometimes joked that they couldn't possibly be related. "You won't believe who I ran into while standing in line to pay."

"Who?" asked Jamil.

"General Sahib. Remember him?"

"Of course! He's the one who single-handedly took out two Soviet tanks during the war in '79."

"Yes, that's the one. Well, he just returned from Afghanistan."

"And?" asked Jamil, his eyebrow cocked, expecting more.

"Well," Uncle Shams said with a sigh, "the news's not so good."

Jamil paused from unwrapping a roll of quarters, and Ariana could see him frown. "Of course it isn't good, Shams," he said. "The war in Afghanistan has been going on since 2001. That's more than six years now."

Ariana threaded packets of saffron onto the rack, remembering how the Americans, French, and forty other countries now had troops stationed in Afghanistan.

Uncle Shams sighed. "Well, President Karzai continues to be a disappointment. Everyone had hoped that after his election he'd bring law and order, security and a sense of peace, after decades of war."

Jamil shook his head, his voice gruff. "He's corrupt and ineffectual—so what can we expect but bad news?"

Ariana noticed Laila stiffen at the talk of Afghanistan and start to rub the locket she wore on a short chain around her neck. Ariana usually ignored all the talk about Afghanistan, since it all seemed so far away and had nothing to do with her life here. But watching Laila freeze like a startled rabbit made her pay attention. Laila's father was still in Afghanistan, finishing up his assignment as a translator with the American army. The position could be dangerous, since many considered translators to be traitors because they helped Americans, whom Afghans considered to be foreign invaders.

"But the news this morning was particularly bad. Twenty-three Koreans passing through Ghazni were taken hostage by the Taliban," said Shams in hushed tones.

Taliban. That was a word Ariana knew well. The Taliban were a group of students who'd taken over Afghanistan in 1996 after the invading Soviets had left. Initially they'd brought order and peace to the country, ending years of civil war. But then they'd become corrupt warlords themselves.

"It's as if history is repeating itself," said Jamil. "The Taliban are gaining in strength, and there's fear they'll soon have a foothold in the country."

Laila dropped a bottle of rose water, and as she scrambled to pick it up, Ariana watched her father and Uncle Shams exchange a guilty look.

"Ariana *jaan*," called out her father. "Why don't you and Laila go get us some coffee at the new café. Get something for yourselves, too."

They're trying to get rid of us, Ariana thought. Recognizing an order when she heard one, Ariana took a twenty-dollar bill from her father and exited the front door. "Come on," she said, grudgingly inviting Laila.

Outside, Ariana paused to wait for her cousin. She noticed the big FOR SALE sign on the dilapidated auto parts warehouse behind Wong Plaza. It had been there for a year, and she hoped that it would be turned into something nice—maybe a park, since it was such an eyesore. Ariana plodded ahead, her flip-flops slapping against the pavement. Laila followed, her long tunic-like *kameez* billowing in the faint breeze. She'd been in the United States for only a few weeks, and although they'd taken her shopping for American clothes—jeans, T-shirts, and sneakers—she still preferred to wear Afghan clothes at home. When they went outside, she put jeans on under her *kameez*.

"Hey, Ariana, how's it going?" called out Mr. Martinez, the owner of Juan More Tacos, the restaurant next door.

"Hi, Mr. Martinez," Ariana said, waving. "Everything's good."

"Who's that with you?" he asked.

"My cousin from Afghanistan," said Ariana. "She's staying with us."

"Great. Well, you can both come by for some chips and salsa when you want."

"Thanks. We will," replied Ariana.

They continued down Wong Plaza, the strip mall where their store was located, anchored on the west end of the plaza. Laila slowed to admire a fuchsia and lime-green sari hanging at Milan's Indian Emporium while Ariana trudged past the Beadery Bead Shoppe and paused at the sale sign at Well-Read Secondhand Books. Her nose pressed against the cool window, she watched Mrs. Smith stack jewel-toned *washi*—thick, handmade Japanese paper—and shimmering square pieces of foil in the front display. Ariana's fingers itched to touch the roughly textured *washi*; at 50 percent off, it would be perfect for making origami.

She gave Mrs. Smith a friendly wave and made a mental note to come back later with her allowance. As she waited for Laila to catch up, she caught a glimpse of her reflection in the window. She wrinkled her nose at the streak of flour in her short, curly hair. Her mother had tried to tame it into a bob, but sadly, it resembled a squat bowl perched on top of her head. A soft T-shirt and fleece sweats enveloped her sturdy frame; the soft fabric was the only type of material that didn't cause her to itch and leave angry red marks on her skin. With a deep sigh she spotted Laila's slender silhouette behind her and pivoted left, waving at Mrs. Kim and her pug, Kimchi, at Koo

Koo Dry Cleaning. She noticed that Hooper's Diner still had a FOR LEASE sign hanging out front.

At the bus stop they paused at the light, waiting for their turn to cross. Laila, ever curious about her surroundings, examined the schedule and the line of posters hanging on the wall. Half a dozen faces stared down from multicolored flyers, all asking the residents of Fremont for their vote in the upcoming elections. The light turned green and the girls hurried across the street to the brand-new strip of stores and the Daily Grind Café. The rich aroma of coffee washed over them as they entered, and luckily, the line was short, so Ariana ordered for her father and uncle.

"Two lattes, please. And—," said Ariana, turning to Laila. "Do you want something?"

Laila shrugged, looking around the store with wide, curious eyes.

Ariana bristled. Laila never talked to her much— she seemed to talk to everyone else in the family, but mostly ignored her. Ariana would have blown Laila off, but her father had told her to get something for *both* of them. "How about a hot chocolate?"

"Hot chocolate?" repeated Laila, a look of confusion on her face. "Chocolate that is hot?"

"You'll like it. Give me two small hot chocolates, too," she added to the barista.

"Should we get something for the boys?" asked Laila.

Ariana had forgotten about them. "And a couple of chocolate chip cookies, please."

While the barista whipped up their order, Laila wandered off to look at the ceramic teapot display. Ariana stood watching a group of men playing chess near the front door and spotted a familiar stooped figure, partially hidden behind the coffee display: it was Lucinda Wong, their landlord. The elderly woman was deep in conversation with a short, burly man with a mane of reddish hair. His back was toward Ariana, so she couldn't make out his face. The barista handed her a cardboard tray with the drinks and cookies, and when Ariana turned back, Mrs. Wong and the man were gone.

Ariana watched the look of wonder spread across Laila's face as they exited. Her cousin had taken a tentative sip of the rich, smooth hot chocolate, and whipped cream lined her upper lip.

Ariana couldn't help but smile. "It's good, huh?"

Laila nodded, licking her lip clean.

Eyes shielded from the bright glare of the sun,

Ariana noticed a sign hanging from the empty building at the east end of Wong Plaza. *That's odd*, she thought. The building had been empty for more than a year, and she'd heard her father say that Lucinda had been trying to rent it out for months. Curious, Ariana walked over to read the notice.

Coming Soon!
Pamir Market
Purveyor of fine foods, halal meat, breads, and Afghan groceries

Ariana stood in front of the sign, her hot chocolate forgotten. A competing Afghan grocery store was opening in the same strip mall as Kabul Corner. *Father and Uncle Shams are not going to like this—not at all*, thought Ariana.

what if no one could hear you?
would they think you had nothing to say?

Melody has a photographic memory. She remembers every word that is spoken around her and every fact she has ever learned. Melody also has cerebral palsy, and is entirely unable to communicate. It's enough to make a girl go out of her mind.

From award-winning author **Sharon M. Draper** comes a book as heartbreaking as it is hopeful, about a girl you'll never forget.